A silver tongue to match his silver eyes, she thought, wishing she had not let him bait her. Mortified, Francesca deliberately gave him her back, which left her staring foolishly at the closed posthouse door.

After a moment, still laughing, he headed in the other direction, the heels of his boots clicking on the oak-wood floor. She could not resist looking around.

He must have been expecting it. Turning, he grinned at her before disappearing into the parlor.

Arrogant coxcomb! He was precisely the sort of man her mother had warned her about—a glib charmer with good looks and bad intentions. Thank heavens she would never see him again. . . .

Books published by The Ballantine Publishing Group are available at quantity discounts on bulk purchases for premium, educational, fund-raising, and special sales use. For details, please call 1-800-733-3000.

FRANCESCA'S RAKE

Lynn Kerstan

FAWCETT CREST • NEW YORK

A Fawcett Crest Book
Published by Ballantine Books
Copyright © 1997 by Lynn Kerstan Horobetz

http://www.randomhouse.com

Library of Congress Catalog Card Number: 96-90985

ISBN 0-449-22766-9

Manufactured in the United States of America

First Edition: June 1997

10   9   8   7   6   5   4   3   2   1

Chapter 1

It is impossible to please all the
world and one's father.
—*Jean de la Fontaine*

Galen Pender, Viscount Clayburn, reined in his
mount on the narrow bridge and seized a calming
breath. Just ahead, the massive limestone walls of
Montford House loomed over the Bedfordshire countryside, reflecting the pale winter sunlight like blocks
of ice.

Wind whipped at his capes as he stared at the home
he rarely visited, except to call on his mother when
his father, the earl, was certain to be elsewhere. For a
moment, scudding clouds cast the estate in shadows,
as if his dark mood had summoned them.

A storm was blowing in—in more ways than one.

Steeling himself for a battle long overdue, Clay
urged his bay to a gallop and rounded the circular
drive in a hail of gravel. Before he could change his
mind, he tossed the reins to a startled gardener, ran
up the marble steps, and pounded on the door.

Javits, butler at Montford House for thirty years,
stepped quickly out of the way as Clay charged into the
house. "Drawing room, milord," he directed. "Lady
Montford is with him."

Clay slowed a trifle. Damn. He did not want his
mother to witness this confrontation. But then, when
did the family ever come together without a brawl?

Montford must have heard the commotion in the

hallway. He was on his feet, one arm resting on the mantelpiece and a look of bored disdain on his face, when Clay erupted into the room.

"How dare you, sir?" Clay closed ground until he was inches from his father, staring straight into silvery eyes so like his own that he had to blink to remind himself he was not looking into a mirror.

The earl lifted a brow. "How dare *you*, Clayburn? To bumble here in all your dirt is inexcusable. Repair to your room, or to the horse trough if you must, and return when you are presentable. Your mother and I shall expect you to be properly announced."

"I d-don't mind, Montford," the countess said in a meek voice. "It is good to see you home, Cl—"

"Be silent!" Montford did not spare her a glance.

Clay turned to his mother and bowed, stricken to see her trembling after the earl's harsh words. "Forgive my poor manners, Mama, but this cannot wait. Perhaps you should leave us for a few minutes."

"She will stay," the earl decreed. "Better she have no illusions about your latest folly and what it has cost me to repair the damage. How could you think to buy colors, Clayburn? Were you intoxicated? But of course you were, to fancy yourself of use to the army, or capable of surviving so much as a week on the Peninsula."

Although his father had scored a direct hit, Clay managed an indifferent shrug. In truth, he'd little idea what was expected of a Light Infantry officer and marveled that the Fifty-second had accepted him in spite of his reputation. "England is at war," he said evenly. "I wished to play my part."

"Nonsense. You imagine yourself gaming and whoring as you do now, but wearing fancy regimentals and out of my reach." Montford smiled his cold smile. "Did

2

you think to escape to Spain, boy? Did you suppose for a moment that I would allow it?"

"I am seven-and-twenty, sir. Old enough to decide for myself. And I bought the commission with my own money."

"Indeed? Since your allowance barely suffices for lodging and food, shall I assume you enjoyed a lucky streak at the hazard tables?"

Clay felt his skin go hot. "Whist, as it happens. And I won with skill, not luck."

"A talent for card-playing?" Montford lifted his quizzing glass. "You astonish me. I had not thought you to have any talent whatsoever. But I do not mean to be unkind. From all accounts the ladies find you irresistible, which will serve us both well when you resign yourself to the business at hand."

Whelping an heir. It always came back to that. Clay glanced at his mother, who gave him a nervous smile of encouragement. He couldn't tell if she meant him to defy the earl or back down.

"Do not hold me accountable for this unpleasant situation, Clayburn." Montford turned his quizzing glass to the countess. "Had this pitiful woman produced another son or two, I would cheerfully disinherit you and leave my fortune to a worthier man. But she failed me, and we all suffer for that."

Clay stripped off his gloves, meaning to fling them at the earl's face, but he heard a choking sound from his mother and looked over at her pale, anxious face. With effort, he curbed his first rash impulse. It would only make him look foolish, after all, and this time he was deadly serious.

"Insult me as you will, sir, but I'll not stand quietly by while you dishonor my mother." He slapped the gloves against his thigh. "Do so again, and I swear we shall come to blows."

3

Dismissing the threat with a wave of his hand, Montford crossed to a side table and lifted the stopper from a decanter. "As you know, I have directed that your commission be resold to some other young buck with more swagger than sense. It required a small gratuity to handle the transaction, so you will be unable to reclaim the full amount."

He poured claret into a glass, sniffed it, and took a long, slow drink. "In fact, I regret to inform you that the funds were misdirected to me. Some error of accounting, no doubt."

Stunned, Clay could only stare at his elegant, hateful father. Still slender and handsome in his late fifties, the earl kept fit by riding to hounds and fencing. He rarely went to London, but his power there was the stuff of legends. It would take only a word in the proper ear to appropriate three thousand pounds rightfully belonging to his son.

Heart pounding, Clay wondered why he still fumbled like a grubby schoolboy in the presence of a man he despised. At least he had trained himself to conceal his emotions, to the point he seldom felt anything deeply, and nothing for very long.

Already his rage had burned out, leaving only a hard knot of determination in his belly. "I accept that you have sliced me out of the army," he said in a calm voice. "But you have no right to steal from me."

"Steal? An absurd and disrespectful accusation, boy. Naturally I shall return the price of your commission, *when* you provide an incentive. And you will definitely need the money, ill begotten as it was, because I am cutting off your allowance."

That was no surprise. Montford had always kept him on a tight leash, financially and in every other way he could devise.

"But there is good news," the earl said with another

of his glacial smiles. "In spite of your rapscallion past, I am willing to give you one last chance to redeem yourself."

"Let me guess." Clay pretended to think it over. "Ah. It can only be the same tune you have sung these last three years. To win myself into that undiscovered country—your good graces—I must marry the Albatross."

For once, he had managed to startle his father. Montford set down his glass and clasped his hands behind his back. "Albatross? One of your obscure jests, no doubt. But yes, I remain convinced that you should wed the young woman I have chosen for you. She will bring to the settlement a large tract of land marching on our estate, along with an enormous dowry. Why you continue to shrink from this ideal marriage eludes me, Clayburn. Once you've got an heir and a spare on her, you may resume your dissipated ways with my blessing."

"Have you considered that she might not have me?"

"Oh, indeed. My contacts in London bring me word of all the reasons why no decent woman of fortune would welcome your addresses. Never doubt I am aware of everything you are up to, Clayburn. But I have some . . . shall we say, influence? If you make an offer, the heiress will surely accept. And you *will* make an offer, if you hope to see another guinea from me. I can make your life very difficult."

"You already have." Clay forced his taut muscles to relax as the glimmer of a plan lit the back of his mind. But he could not work out the details in his father's presence. The earl sucked all the air out of the room, making it hard to breathe.

Only the goal remained clear—freedom from Montford's iron-fisted control and a touch of revenge to seal his independence. This time he meant to defy his father and win.

And he must find a safe haven for his mother. That goal immediately shot to the top of his list. Until now, he had failed the only person he had ever loved, shaming her when he meant to shame the earl.

No more. While he rather enjoyed his notoriety as London's most profligate rake, he could change. He *would* change.

But to best the earl, he must be cold, deliberate, and unrelenting. He must learn to use his father's own weapons—cunning and deceit—against him.

"Well?" Montford made an impatient gesture. "Gone napping, Clayburn?"

"Merely devising a compromise, sir. What if—"

"I do not believe in compromise," Montford interrupted, scowling.

No, Clay thought angrily, his father expected capitulation. Unclenching his fists, Clay produced a smile like the ones his father had perfected—smiles that could freeze molten lead. "Hold off the allowance if you choose, sir, but give me the money from the commission. It is rightfully mine. In return, I swear to marry within the year."

"The heiress. I forget her name. Agree to marry *her*."

Unwilling to break his word, even to a man he loathed, Clay fumbled for a loophole. "I certainly agree to meet her when I return from London. Shall we say two months from now?"

"Why not immediately? What is the point of delay?"

"You have made it necessary with your interference. I must cancel orders for uniforms, horses, weapons, and the like. Or have you already seen to that?"

For the first time, Montford looked ill at ease. "I suppose you must give up your rooms and attend to business before resettling here. But do so in one month, not two. Otherwise, I'll not give you a penny."

How absurd to do battle over a few thousand pounds with so much else at stake. Clay wanted to tell his father, graphically, what he could do with the money. It would make a good exit line. But he was through with dramatic flourishes. And he truly required funds just to survive while he set his tentative plan in motion. At the moment, he had thirty guineas to his name and owed several times that amount to his landlord and assorted creditors.

Fortunately, the earl expected him to beg. With a bit of fake humility and a few vague promises, he could win seed money to finance his new plan. "Tailors and gunsmiths will expect something for their labor," he said, pasting a downcast look on his face. "And I have other debts. If only for the sake of your own reputation, they must be paid."

Montford released a heavy sigh. "Oh, very well. One thousand pounds, on your promise to marry within the year. Contact my solicitor when you reach London. But you will return here in four weeks, prepared to honor your vow, or I shall break you. Trust me on that."

Lacking ammunition for a battle of ultimatums, Clay choked down a few vulgar retorts and bowed curtly.

With a gesture of dismissal, the earl settled in his chair beside the hearth, put on his spectacles, and picked up the book he had been reading. In the firelight, his thick white hair shone like a halo.

Clay regarded his father's aloof profile with contempt. All of a year since he had been home, but to the earl he was of no more consequence than a tradesman. Their business completed, the arctic silence he remembered from childhood enveloped them again.

7

Forcing a warm smile to his cold lips, Clay turned to his mother and offered his arm.

"Surely you are not leaving so soon," she protested in a low voice when they reached the foyer. "Please, Galen," she said, using her favored name for Clay. "At least stay the night."

"I am too angry, Mama. Forgive me, but it is better that I depart immediately. Besides, Jerry and Bertie are in Thurleigh with the carriage, expecting me within the hour. We plan to be well on the road to London before nightfall."

She lowered her head. "You must not keep your friends waiting, of course."

"Ah, Mama." He raised her chin gently with his finger, remorse clutching at his heart. Her pale blue eyes shimmered with tears, but she had learned never to weep openly. Her husband despised weakness of any sort.

With a groan, Clay drew her into a tight embrace. "In a few weeks I shall be here again," he promised. "And very soon, you will have a daughter-in-law and grandchildren to cosset. I expect you to leave this mausoleum and come live with us, so do not think to make excuses. In this matter, neither you nor the earl will overrule me."

She understood, he knew, as she stood on tiptoe to kiss his cheek. Probably she understood more than he imagined. A wonder that she had never lost faith in him, despite his rackety life. While he rebelled against his father, she endured.

Her quiet courage fired his resolve. Somehow, he would make a new home for her. If all else failed, he would even wed the Albatross.

But for now, he must reach London with all possible speed. By reselling the commission and making no secret of it, Montford had publicly, and quite deliberately, disgraced his son. And in response, Clay meant to do the last thing his father expected of him. He would stay the course. For however long it took, he would deflect gossip with charm and wit, hold his head high, and ride out the scandal.

"Good-bye, Mama," he said, giving her one last hug. "When next we meet, I shall have good news for you."

Stepping back, she fixed him with a clear-eyed gaze. "Only tell me you are happy and in love, Galen. Nothing else will do."

Chapter 2

They drink and dance by their own light;
They drink and revel all the night.
                                    —*Abraham Cowley*

"I wish this were over and done with, Papa." Francesca pulled a chair close to the enormous canopied bed and sat beside the frail man nestled against a bank of pillows.

Melchior Childe, Duke of Sotherton, stroked her cheek with a gnarled thumb. "You will return to plague me soon enough, Cesca. In spite of the disagreeable task that takes you there, London will do you a world of good."

For his sake, she rallied a show of enthusiasm. "I expect the booksellers to declare a holiday after I buy out half their stock. And I long to visit the Royal Gallery and the museums. Maria Beaton says in her letters that there are lectures about science and art nearly every day. She has even promised to secure an invitation to one of Lady Holland's dinners."

The duke frowned. "Never you mind the political debates and stuffy museums, little bluestocking. You must dance and make merry. I insist upon it."

"Scarcely *little*, Papa. But fear not. I shall be present at every rout and ball to which we are invited. Until the girls are betrothed, of course, at which time I'll gladly wash my hands of them and come home to pluck rare sirloin and buttered lobster from your greedy fingers."

He shuddered dramatically. "I have so few pleasures these days, and you scheme to deprive me of every one. Even so, I shall miss you dreadfully while you are gone. My brother has exceeded all bounds this time, snatching you away to chaperone his daughters and hounding me to pay for their come-out."

"What a clanker!" Francesca broke out laughing. "As if Bromley Childe ever rubbed two thoughts together in a single hour. I know very well you engineered this absurd plan as an excuse to propel me into Society."

"True enough, I put the flea in Bromley's ear. But how else was I to rid myself of the tyrant who feeds me pap and hides my cigars? For the next several months, you can apply that iron will to my nieces." He poked her on the shoulder. "Be careful of the birdwit, Cesca. Runs ahead of the fox, that one."

Francesca nodded ruefully. "If only Bromley were not coming with us. He permits Livvy to do whatever she wishes, and I dare not overrule him."

"You can, and you must. Only remember who holds the purse strings. Bromley cannot afford to present his daughters without my support, and I have put you in charge. Buy expensive wardrobes for yourself and the girls, stage the most lavish ball of the Season, and do me proud. Not a farthing to my brother, though, under any circumstances. He will only game it away."

"I promise. And I shall apply to you constantly for advice, which you will send by return post or—"

"Yes, yes, I shall write, if only to assure you there is no need to come flying home. But tell me happy stories in your letters, *carina*. I wish to hear of your beaux and how you have taken the ton by storm." He took her hand and pressed it to his heart. "Most of all, I want to hear that you have fallen in love."

Beneath the soft nightshirt, she felt his sunken

chest and the erratic throb of his pulse. *Oh, Papa.* She blinked against a sudden wash of tears. *How can I leave you?*

But how could she deny him, especially after he had so cleverly backed her into a corner?

Papa cared not a whit for what became of the Sotherton dynasty after his death, so long as his precious library survived. It was willed to her, and she knew every volume and manuscript as if they were her brothers and sisters.

He had compiled a list of books for her to find and purchase in London, but that was only another excuse to send her away. In truth, Papa did not want her here to watch him die.

But the doctor felt certain he would survive at least another year or more, and she fully intended to return within a few weeks.

Moreover, she had a special reason of her own to go to London. Ever since she could remember, Papa had searched high and low for a book he longed to possess. And just last month, Maria Beaton had written with exciting news. The slender volume of Petrarch's sonnets, illustrated by a nameless artist who might have known the poet, had appeared in a list of items up for auction.

Francesca intended to buy it for her stepfather, to thank him for all he had given her—a home, security for the future, and, most of all, his unfailing love. The book was trivial in comparison, a gesture only, but he would understand.

She also meant to see that the Sotherton title survived the scapegrace brother who stood to inherit. Bromley was already beyond hope, but his son, safely installed at Oxford, might yet become a worthy Duke of Sotherton.

And, too, Bromley's daughters deserved a chance to marry well. Unless she escorted them to London for the Season, Ann and Livvy would eventually dwindle into spinsterhood. No eligible man had ever shown his face in Rutlandshire, so far as she knew.

For herself, Francesca had no illusions. She was one-and-thirty, taller than most men, and better educated. If all that failed to spook a potential suitor, her illegitimate birth to an Italian commoner would turn the trick.

Even so, she would most likely be courted by a fortune hunter or two. One bidder had already applied for her hand, but only because it happened to be attached to a parcel of land he wanted. And he refused to take no for an answer.

Letters arrived regularly, but they were not even written by the man she was expected to marry. Instead, the Earl of Montford conducted negotiations with the Duke of Sotherton, as if the bride and groom had nothing whatever to say in the matter.

What kind of man would allow his father to sell him off in a business transaction? she wondered. Lord Clayburn must be thoroughly spineless.

Not that she cared in the least, because she'd no intention of accepting a marriage of convenience. Why would she want a man ordering her about and spending her money? With financial independence, a consuming love of books, and a wide circle of penfriends, what more could she need?

Still, there were those pesky dreams, in the cold hours before dawn, when she fretted alone in her bed. Perfectly understandable, she supposed, but most annoying.

"Italian women are passionate," her mother had warned when she began her monthly bleeding. After explaining how a female body changed and why, she had spoken with an urgency that forever sealed her words in Francesca's mind.

"I shall never regret yielding to the Englishman," Renalda had said in her honeyed Italian accent. "Because of him, I have my precious daughter. But passion without love nearly always ends in disaster. Had Melchior not rescued us from the streets, we would surely be dead by now. So take care, beloved. When a man tempts you, and when your body longs for his touch, trust only your mind and your heart."

At the time, Francesca had had no earthly idea what her mother had meant, although her understanding had improved since. Most of her information was derived from books, though, because she knew better than to place confidence in anything her body had to say—even when it was practically shouting.

Never mind that it squirmed on the sheets at night, wanting what a healthy female body was bound to want. That same body also sniffled with colds and got rashes when she ate shellfish. Who could account for what a body did?

"My dear?" The duke tugged at her long braid. "Did all this talk of love cause you to go mute?"

"In fact, it set me to air-dreaming about London." Mustering a smile, she told him what he wanted to hear. "I shall dazzle all the eligible bachelors and break hearts by the score, until I find the man of my dreams. Then I shall bring him here for the most lavish wedding celebration in Rutlandshire history, and the Duke of Sotherton will lead me down the aisle."

He squeezed her hand. "You are humoring me again, Cesca. Do not think I fail to mark your stratagems. Although my body is failing bit by bit, my brain still functions perfectly well."

"Of course it does. You are the wisest man I have ever known."

"Faint praise, since I am virtually the only man

14

you know. But make yourself useful one more time and pour me a glass of brandy. One for you, too."

"Papa—"

"Go!"

Unable to quarrel with him during these last few minutes together, she went to the sideboard and measured a bare half inch of brandy into a pair of glasses. One driblet would do no harm. Besides, he kept a flask under his pillow, to use when the pain assailed him at night. They both pretended she didn't know.

The duke had pulled himself straighter on the pillows. Accepting his glass with courtly grace, he patted the spot on the bed near his waist where he wanted her to sit. "I never look at you without thinking of your mother, *carina*. You are so much like her—beautiful, intelligent, and blessed with her loving spirit."

"Don't forget her temper."

His eyes grew misty, and Francesca knew he was about to launch into a familiar tale. She leaned into the circle of his arm, trying as always to remember what he described. But she had been three years old at the time, half-starved, and probably terrified. She recalled nothing of how he had met her mother. Indeed, if not for the duke's stories and for her mama's vague descriptions of their hardscrabble life in Italy, she would swear she had been born here at Sotherton Manor.

Her real father was British, a navy lieutenant whose name Mama took to her grave ten years ago. She had said he died of cholera before they could marry, but more likely he had seduced and then abandoned her.

Perhaps he was dead, or perhaps he now had a family of his own. Francesca didn't care one way or the other. With all her heart, she loved the man who had adopted her and raised her as if she were his natural child.

The duke had come to his favorite part of the tale, which Francesca could almost recite with him word for word. "I nearly tripped over her there in the street. Just another beggar, I thought. Naples was full of them. I tossed her a coin and tried to move on, but you jumped up and kicked me on the shin. I still don't know why."

"Nor do I," she said on cue. "Except that I was born a brat."

"Poor Renalda. She was so embarrassed, pulling you away and apologizing in Italian. I understood little of what she said, but when I looked into her clear dark eyes, I fell head over tail in love. Only imagine, pumpkin. I was lost, trying to get somewhere or t'other, and God led me into the alley where I met my wife and daughter."

"God was watching out for us all," she affirmed dutifully.

She wanted to believe that. Could a mere coincidence change so many lives? And yet, the cynic in her refused to accept the possibility of divine intervention in everyday human affairs. The occasional miracle, perhaps, when the Lord saw fit. But in general, people were expected to struggle on as best they could.

"Again you humor an old man's folly," he said gently. "Thank you for listening, and forgive me for prosing on. I relive my past and plot your future, which must surely grate on your nerves." He lifted his glass. "Shall we make a toast?"

"Aye, sir. To what shall we drink?"

"Why, to love. What else matters?" He swallowed his brandy in a single gulp, coughed, and took the handkerchief she pulled from her sleeve, pressing it against his mouth.

Then she touched her glass to her lips, preserving the moment for his sake. "To love."

"But I don't *wish* to stop!" Livvy kicked her foot against the leather squabs, barely missing Francesca's knee. "Father, tell her we must go on."

Francesca ignored Bromley's muttered protest and spoke to the shivering footman peering at her through the carriage window. His eyelashes were crusted with ice.

"Tell the driver to pull in at the next posthouse," she said firmly. "And watch for the baggage coach. I fear it may have got stuck. If it fails to catch up, we must send help."

The footman disappeared into the swirling snow, and soon the carriage resumed its slow progress, swaying against the buffeting winds.

"We'll never get to London at this rate," Livvy whined. "Move over, Ann. You are taking up more than half the seat."

"I'm sorry." Ann scrunched even closer to the paneled door and smiled at Francesca. "Livvy is a restless traveler."

Francesca swallowed a scorching reply. She was fond of sweet, conciliatory Ann, although the girl really ought to find her backbone. As for Livvy, Francesca already wanted to strangle the wretched chit.

It was Livvy who had insisted they set out that morning despite the snow flurries that had already begun when the Sotherton coaches arrived at Lord Bromley's house. They should have waited until the weather cleared before proceeding to London, but Livvy had thrown a tantrum right there in the driveway.

Now, because Francesca had given in, the carriage would likely be mired in the drifting snow before they could reach the safety of an inn. The hot bricks under her feet had long since gone cold, and her fingers and toes felt like slivers of ice. What must the driver and footman be suffering?

Next to her, Bromley wrapped himself in a heavy blanket and soon began to snore. Just as well, Francesca thought. Awake, he was only slightly less irritating than Livvy.

The wan winter light slowly faded, and when the sun disappeared altogether, even the body heat of four passengers could not warm the carriage. Ann and Livvy forgot their quarrel and huddled together, faces invisible under fur-lined cloaks.

Francesca tried to sleep, but her mind whirled with visions of disaster. This nightmare journey was all her fault. Papa had advised her to ignore Bromley's wishes, but already she had let him overrule her judgment. It would not happen again, she resolved. From now on, she would make the decisions.

Pulling out her watch, she looked at the time and grimaced. Nearly midnight. Where the devil were they? She rubbed frost from the window and peered outside, but windblown snow had frozen in a thick sheet on the glass. She could see nothing.

Moments later, the coach shuddered to a halt.

Dear God! Swallowing a rush of panic, she waited for word from the footman.

After an endless minute, she heard him stabbing at the encrusted ice on the carriage door. When he broke through and raised the latch, icy wind screamed into the compartment.

"P-posthouse," he shouted through chattering teeth.

Gathering her cloak around her, Francesca accepted his arm and stepped into snow up to her knees.

Light streamed from the posthouse windows, and she saw a lóng line of coaches parked in a row. Most wore a thick mantle of white. A pair of ostlers had just detatched horses from another carriage, the latest to arrive, and were leading them toward the stable.

"I can make it from here," she told the footman. "See to the others."

Livvy jumped out next to her. "Why are we stopping again?"

Francesca whirled around. "Help your father and Ann to the door while I go ahead to make arrangements. And if you question why we are stopping, here is the answer." Scooping up a handful of snow, she mashed it into Livvy's startled face.

Laughter and music blared from the taproom, louder than the screeching wind. Through the window, Francesca saw a man playing a fiddle. She tramped to the door and let herself in.

Three travelers stood in the passageway, facing away from her, their caped greatcoats dusted with fresh snow. She could not see the man who was addressing them.

" . . . reserved for families with children, you understand. Can't have 'em running underfoot, what with all this crowd."

"A private parlor, then?" said a low baritone voice.

"Got three, but they ain't private tonight. Not even for Quality, milord. The one in front is for the ladies, and the middle room for anyone who cares to use it. I expect you gentlemen will prefer the rear parlor, where I've set up tables with cards and dice to help you pass the time. A servant will bring you a meal there, unless you prefer to eat in the dining hall."

"We'll take supper in the parlor, thank you, along with several bottles of your best claret."

"I'll see to it immediately. Straight ahead, then. Last door to the left." As the men walked away, stripping off their coats and gloves, the proprietor caught sight of Francesca by the door and gave her a welcoming smile. "Traveling alone, ma'am? Wait just a moment, please. I'll be right back to attend you."

"B-but . . . " Her voice faded off. Time enough to correct him when the others arrived.

One of the men turned then, acknowledging her with a slight bow.

At first she pretended not to see him run his gaze slowly from the toes of her wet half-boots to the brim of her drooping bonnet. *Diàvolo!* No man had ever looked at her that way, as if he could see right through her sable-lined cape and woolen dress.

All too aware of a flush rising to her cold cheeks, she planted her feet solidly and gave him back eye for eye.

Within seconds, she regretted her boldness. No man ought to be that handsome, or make it clear he knew that she had noticed. But try as she might, she could not look away from his eyes.

Until now, she had not imagined that eyes came in that color. Blue, hazel, gray, brown, even black. But pure silver? She wrenched her gaze to his dark hair, sleek and wet from the snow, took swift note of smiling lips over a firm chin, and finally realized she was actually looking *up* at a man.

He stood nearly a head taller, and seemed to fill the narrow passageway with his broad shoulders and long legs. "You should not have been left here alone," he said affably. "Shall I keep you company until the innkeeper returns? Better yet, why not join me for supper?"

Stunned, Francesca gaped at him for a moment before snapping her mouth shut. Join him for supper indeed! No gentleman would make such an offer to a lady he had never met.

But then, he was clearly *not* a gentleman, and she could only imagine what he thought of her. "Thank you," she said curtly, "but I do not require your assistance."

"Are you certain?" His smile widened. "It will be a long night, I fear, and my friends will be glad of someone new to converse with. After too many hours together in a coach, we are heartily sick of one another."

"I'm not surprised."

He laughed. "*Touché*. We would be dull company indeed for a goddess."

Goddess? A silver tongue to match his silver eyes, she thought, wishing she had not let him bait her. Mortified, Francesca deliberately gave him her back, which left her staring foolishly at the closed posthouse door.

After a moment, still laughing, he headed in the other direction, the heels of his boots clicking on the oak-wood floor. She could not resist looking around.

He must have been expecting it. Turning, he grinned at her before disappearing into the parlor.

Arrogant coxcomb! He was precisely the sort of man her mother had warned her about—a glib charmer with good looks and bad intentions. Thank heavens she would never see him again.

The proprietor emerged from the taproom as Livvy burst into the foyer, followed by her father. Ann limped beside him, clinging to Bromley's arm.

"I twisted my ankle when I jumped from the coach," she explained, "but it hurts only a little."

"Have you secured our rooms?" Bromley stomped snow from his boots. "Who's in charge here? I want a hot bath and a bottle of brandy."

The proprietor moved forward, ignoring Bromley to take Ann's other arm. "This way, ladies. When you are nestled right and tight by the fire, I'll send Mrs. Hoyt to look at the young miss's injury. M'name's

Josiah Hoyt, and you are welcome to the Rose and Thistle."

He led them to a small room already crowded with women, some of them stretched on mattresses that had been laid out on the floor. Two wing chairs were angled by the fireplace, and Mr. Hoyt quickly offered a free meal if the ladies who occupied them cared to adjourn to the dining room. They were gone in a flash.

Francesca gave him a grateful smile. "Thank you. I shall pay for their dinners, of course."

"Oh, I'll be makin' plenty of blunt tonight, this bein' the only posthouse for ten miles either direction. You just settle back and let old Josiah take care of you."

Old Josiah was a marvel. In the next hour, Francesca watched him handle fretful customers with bluff good humor while his staff served up bowls of spicy beef stew, chunks of crusty bread, and wedges of cheese.

Mrs. Hoyt brought a pot of steaming water for Ann to soak her ankle and gave her a pillow to support her foot. The ankle was slightly swollen, but after dinner Ann was able to walk down the hall to use the commode.

Livvy, still in a huff, had long since disappeared with her father into the taproom. Francesca suspected she ought to go after her, but it was nearly midnight and the ladies' parlor had gone quiet except for a few murmured conversations and soft snoring from the corner. Dragging a recalcitrant Livvy there would disturb everyone's rest.

Francesca leaned back in the chair, smoke from the fireplace stinging her eyes. She let them drift shut. In a few minutes she would go check on Livvy. Really she would.

* * *

"Cesca!" Ann tugged at her arm. "Wake up."

The first thing she saw was the mantel clock. Good heavens! It had gone past three. How had she slept so long? Francesca sat up and looked at Ann's worried face. "What is wrong? Does your ankle—"

"It's fine. I went looking for Livvy, but I cannot find her. Or Father. They aren't in the taproom."

"You shouldn't be wandering about on your own," Francesca chided gently, "especially on that sore foot. Sit, please, and wait here while I track them down."

Except for the rowdy taproom, the Rose and Thistle was filled with sleeping travelers. Servants had curled up on the floor, and she saw her own driver and footman snoozing in a corner of the dining hall.

Tiptoeing around the prone bodies, she returned to the passageway. Josiah had said there were three private parlors, so she tried the second door and scanned the crowded room. A few people turned in her direction, scowling at the disturbance. Softly, she closed the door and swore under her breath.

She should have guessed immediately. The last parlor was reserved for gentlemen, "with dice and cards to pass the time." Naturally her uncle would find his way there, with Livvy in tow if she insisted. As she would. Dear Lord, at this rate the child would be ruined before they even got to London.

Guilt soured Francesca's tongue. She had allowed Livvy to slip the leash, and now there would be the devil to pay.

Steeling herself, she went to the last door on the left and cracked it open. The stench of cigars, stale wine, and sweat hit her like a fist. *Còrpo di Bacco!* How could anyone remain in that room? A blanket of smoke hung over the tables, and she could scarcely see to the opposite wall.

23

"Come on in, precious!" called a voice to her right. "Don't be shy." A loud chorus approved the invitation.

Francesca drew herself to her full height and stepped inside, looking over the crowd until she spotted Bromley huddled at a table with three other men. Pretending she did not hear the catcalls and insults aimed at her, she strode calmly across the room.

Livvy was wedged between her father and the silver-eyed man, her knee pressed against his thigh. She held a glass of wine.

"Hullo, Cesca," she said, her voice slurred. "I'm learnin' to play whist."

Francesca took a deep breath and glanced at a long-fingered hand resting on the table next to a large stack of guineas and banknotes. The man had removed his coat and untied his cravat. In the light from a chandelier directly overhead, his white shirtsleeves and silver-threaded waistcoat shimmered through the cloud of smoke.

What effrontery, to dally with Olivia right in front of her father! Even now he made no move to withdraw his leg. The sight of his muscular thigh against Livvy's knee made Francesca want to throttle him with a blunt object.

She moved to Livvy's side and leaned over to whisper in her ear. "Come with me now, in silence, or we shall not continue on to London."

"Ah," the man said, his voice amused. "The ladies have a secret. Shall we compel them to share it with us?"

Compel? Francesca lifted her chin and glared directly into his silver-mirror eyes.

"Whoever the devil you are, sir, I suggest you mind your own blasted business!"

Chapter 3

Therefore who her will conquer ought to be
At least as full of love and wit as she.
                              —*Charles Cotton*

Clay sat back in his chair, laughing.

What a termagant! But not at all a garden-variety shrew. Immediately after swearing at him, she had blushed a delicious shade of pink. Enchanted, he watched her bend again to whisper in the tipsy girl's ear and take the wineglass from her hand.

Clearly she was not traveling alone, as he had thought when he spoke to her in the passageway. Flirted with her, truth be told, but more from habit than attraction. Wet and bedraggled under her heavy cape and sagging bonnet, she had appealed only to his deepest male instincts.

But those instincts had been right on target, as usual. Now he could see what the cape and hat had concealed—a ripe, full-breasted figure under her drab woolen dress, a smooth complexion, and a magnificent pair of flashing black eyes. Clay ran one finger under his collar. The room had gone a great deal warmer in the last few minutes.

For all her startling beauty, he suspected she was employed as governess or chaperone to the chit who had plagued him for the last three hours. Since there was no wedding ring on her finger, she could not be Bromley Childe's wife. Another of his children, perhaps?

But those exotic eyes and the long black hair escaping the single braid down her back set her apart from the vapid gamester and his annoying blond daughter. A mystery, this vastly seductive woman.

And he loved mysteries, especially when they came packaged in soft female flesh.

At last the goddess managed to pry Miss Childe from the table, and loud protests from the besotted men rang out as she hauled her young charge from the room. Clay tried to catch her eye, but she never looked back.

Unfortunate. But she had been aware of him when they met in the passageway. Deliciously aware.

He understood women, having made a study of them since his voice changed, and this one was a banked fire. Or an explosion waiting for the right man to light her fuse. Were he not too squiffy from the claret, and the inn so crowded, he would strike that flame this very night.

The card game had long since grown dull, so he gathered his winnings and stood. "Deal me out, gentlemen. I require a breath of fresh air."

"You can't quit now," Childe protested. "My luck is bound to turn."

"Then you must recoup your losses from someone else, sir." Clay pulled on his coat. "May I suggest you try another game? You have no skill at whist."

With relief, he stepped into the dim passageway and closed the door behind him, pausing to enjoy his first smoke-free breath in several hours. Two bottles of claret had turned his legs to noodles. Leaning against the wall for support, he waited for his head to stop spinning.

Decadence would be a great deal more pleasurable if it could be indulged in cleaner surroundings with more agreeable companions than Bromley Childe. And without the inevitable hangover.

Mostly without the self-disgust that usually haunted him until he drank enough to stop caring. Lately, though, even liquor and a succession of delightful bedmates could not still the inner voice that nagged for his attention.

Fool! You are throwing away your life.

Drawing himself erect, he took a few tentative steps down the long hall and stopped again. Just ahead, the termagant had the widgeon plastered against the wall. He slipped into a dark spot between two bronze candelabra to watch.

The widgeon stamped her foot. "Father didn't mind. And he is almost a duke."

"Not *yet*!" The air fairly sizzled. "How dare you, Olivia?"

Her voice lowered then, and Clay had to settle for looking at her. Gilded by the flickering light, she was altogether splendid. An earthbound goddess, tall and regal and imperious, with a body shaped for pleasure.

"One more trick like this one," she said in a loud hiss, "and the only offer you can expect from a man will not include a wedding ring. If you are determined to scandalize your family, confine yourself to the farmhands in Rutlandshire. I shall whisk you there in an instant if you shame the duke again, as you have done this night."

"That means you'll have to go back, too," the chit said defiantly.

"My greatest wish is to return home this very moment. Pray remember that, whenever you are tempted to misbehave. I agreed to be your chaperone against my will, and I shall seize any excuse to end this nightmare."

"That's because you are old and dried up and not

27

likely to have any fun! Do you even know *how* to have fun? Tonight a handsome viscount paid me considerable attention. You are jealous, Francesca, because that will never happen to you."

Francesca? A lovely name. If only he knew the rest of it. But did that little blond witch mistake his tolerance of her outrageous behavior for genuine interest? Clay had not meant to interfere, but Francesca's stunned silence after the bruising attack rang in his ears. A soundless cry of pain, he realized, surprised that he had heard it.

Angry for her sake, he lifted his shoulders away from the wall and strode down the passageway, feigning a look of surprise when he reached the two women. "Ah, we meet again. Forgive me if I have interrupted a private coze."

Livvy gave him a cheeky grin. "You are most welcome, sir. I am being read a lecture."

"Indeed?" He lifted a brow. "Perhaps you have earned it. The gaming tables are no place for a young lady, Miss Childe, but of course, you know that. Fortunately, no one will remark that you joined your father this night. The inn was crowded with stranded travelers, and we all took refuge where we could find a shred of space."

"Y-yes." Even Olivia could not mistake the censure in his voice. "Excuse me, please. I must find my sister." With a swift curtsy, she fled down the hall.

And good riddance! Now he had the goddess all to himself. Clay opened his mouth to say something charming, one of the practiced compliments that never failed to beguile a woman, but his tongue stuck to the roof of his mouth.

Francesca was regarding him with curious astonishment, as if she had just seen a pig stand on its hind legs and recite a sonnet.

To be sure, she could expect no good of him after what she had observed in the gaming room. In fact, she had caught him in one of his better moments—partly sober, no woman on his lap—which spoke volumes about his general behavior.

"Truly, I am not so b-bad as you think." Damn! Could he possibly have said that more awkwardly?

Her eyes narrowed.

"Be sure I have no carnal designs on the young lady," he continued like a stampeded mule. "Whatever her misapprehensions, or yours, Miss Childe is perfectly safe."

"I shall see to that," Francesca replied sharply. "But when gentlemen—and I use that term with no certainty it applies to you—are in their cups, impetuous young ladies are easily led to mistake their intentions. You are older and wiser than Olivia, sir. In future, pray recall how easily a woman's reputation is damaged beyond repair."

This particular woman might have taken lessons in intimidation from his father. Impressed, Clay lifted his arms in a gesture of surrender. "I was careless and irresponsible. In truth, I paid no attention whatever to the girl. But I should have sent her away."

To his relief, Francesca melted slightly. "She is a handful, to be sure, and I am at fault for letting her escape my protection. Thank you for setting her straight a few minutes ago. She got a bit above herself in the gaming room, but you brought her down to earth."

"I hope so." Clay grinned. "If I never see her again, she will not be missed. I cannot say the same for you, however. Your name is Francesca?"

With a startled look, she backed up a step. "Did Brom—Lord Bromley tell you that? Or were you listening to my conversation with Livvy?"

"Does it matter? I wish to make your acquaintance, and I would do so in proper fashion were there anyone to introduce us. But we are both snowbound and alone together, so perhaps we can dispense with the formalities." He bowed. "I am Galen Pender, Viscount Clayburn."

He had rather hoped she would be impressed. How many chaperones won the attention of a viscount, after all?

The more fool he. Francesca's eyes went round as moons, as if the devil himself had sprung up in front of her. Before he could react, she spun around and vanished into the ladies' parlor.

What was *that* about? He stared at the empty passageway, unable to credit that the mere sound of his name had sent her scampering. Surely reports of his unsavory reputation had not reached all the way to Rutlandshire. He'd never set foot in the tiny rural county, and had the impression no one lived there but cows and sheep.

Another mystery to solve, when he sobered up.

Clay aimed himself at the main door and wobbled on shaky legs into the cold air. The storm had passed, and someone had shoveled the path to the stable. Overhead, Orion blazed in the clear black sky.

After finding a dark place at the side of the inn to relieve himself, he trudged through the knee-deep snow toward a copse of oak. The leafless branches, crusted with ice, glittered in the starlight.

The silence and the stark beauty made him feel painfully alive. Achingly alone.

He wanted so many things that eluded his reach. Or he assumed they did. He wanted, but he didn't know what he wanted most, so he never tried for anything important. Only good times and irresponsibility, which left him unsatisfied and useless. Above all, useless.

Even now, with a goal in mind, he scarcely knew where to begin. Clay picked up a handful of snow and let it sift through his fingers. There would be no easy escape from his father's tyranny, so he might as well resign himself to the inevitable.

Marriage.

Not to the Albatross, God forbid. Damned if he would marry solely to bring a few acres of land into the Montford holdings. All he knew about the heiress was her age, which the earl had let slip in an unguarded moment.

One-and-thirty, for pity's sake. Four years older than he. An heiress unwed at that advanced age could only be an antidote of the first order. Besides, she was his father's choice, which made her the last woman in the universe he would take to wife.

But if he married someone else . . .

The ill-formed plan at the back of his mind began to take shape. The earl had the influence to buy back his son's commission in the army, but surely he could not annul a consummated marriage. And if the bride were of no consequence, a cit or a foreigner, so much the better.

Clay rubbed his hands together, feeling an unfamiliar surge of excitement. He imagined himself drawing up in a coach at Montford House with a wholly unsuitable wife and thumbing his nose at the earl.

Money would be no problem once he married, even when Montford inevitably deprived him of everything that was not entailed to the legitimate heir. His grandmother had settled a fortune on him, currently managed by the earl, which would revert to Clay when he produced a son or daughter. Blessedly, women were not so fussy as men about the gender of children when they made out their wills.

It wasn't as though he had the option of marrying

for love, if such a thing existed. Now and again he tried to picture a happy home with a wife he adored and a gaggle of children clinging to his legs, but the vision never formed clearly enough for him to believe in it.

Reality was the trap his father had set for him, and his plan was to escape it. All he needed was a bride.

And tonight, by sheerest luck, he had stumbled upon the perfect woman. Francesca. A hot-tempered beauty for his own pleasure, and a wife without fortune or lineage to gall his father. True, she had a poor opinion of him at the moment, but what spinster chaperone would not leap at the chance to marry into the aristocracy?

The nagging voice at the back of his head said, *This one.*

Ah, well. He relished the challenge of bringing a goddess to earth. And he wanted to bed her. The intensity of his desire astounded him. He had felt lust . . . he often felt lust . . . but never an overwhelming attraction to a specific woman. How ironic to feel his body grow hard just thinking of the most straitlaced female he had ever met.

On fire with more enthusiasm than he had felt in years, Clay went to the stable and instructed a sleepy ostler to make his carriage ready to depart at first hint of daylight. Even with a blanket of snow covering the road, he would make faster time than the travelers slogging through grimy slush later in the day.

In high spirits, he returned to the inn and rallied his friends. The Quest was under way!

Feet propped on hot bricks, steaming pork pies in their hands, Bertram and Jeremy Porter stared blankly when Clay outlined his plan.

"You can't mean it," Bertie said.

"Are you queer in the attic?" Jerry fell forward and then back against the squabs as the carriage made its halting way through the drifted snow. "Marry a nobody? The earl will hang you up by your nether parts."

"He'll want to," Clay agreed. "Which is the whole point. Or a good part of it," he added with strict honesty. The Porter brothers had been his boon companions since his early days at Eton, and he rarely lied to them. But this time he meant to keep a few secrets, including his peculiar obsession with the goddess. They would not understand. For that matter, neither did he.

"If I don't marry someone else, Montford will leg-shackle me to the Albatross. Better a wife of my own choosing, and best if she is the last woman he would welcome into the family. No money, no rank, no property, nothing but a certificate of marriage to put an end to all his plots."

Bertie frowned. "Albatross? What the devil is an albatross?"

"A large bird," Clay explained slowly. Bertie was none too bright, even when not in his cups, but his sweet nature made him a favorite in Society. "In a poem by Mister Coleridge, a dead albatross is suspended around the neck of the sailor who killed it, as punishment for his sin."

"Aha!" Bertie waved his pork pie. "See what comes of reading about birds who cock up their toes, Claws. Whatever birds cock up. The earl is trying to marry you off to an heiress, which is no bad thing in my opinion. But you figure she is an albatross before you even meet her." He took a bite of pie and spoke through a mouthful of thick crust. "Me, I know a female from a dead bird. Prob'ly because I never read poems."

Clay grinned at Jerry. Amiable Bertie had survived

Oxford only because his brother had written all his papers and exams. And they were both spared expulsion because Clay took full blame for the pranks they devised and pulled off together. Only he had been rusticated after they herded a flock of sheep into Christchurch Chapel, precisely when the dean was addressing a congregation of wealthy benefactors.

"What's the difference between marrying an albatross and a servant?" Jerry asked reasonably. "Either way, you are shackled to a wife you don't want. Why not bite the bullet and make peace with the earl? He will hound you forever if you continue to defy him, and it's not likely you will ever win."

When Clay frowned, Jerry gave him back an innocent smile. "I say take the albatross, sire an heir on her, and come back to London with us. That's the sensible thing. Your life can proceed as it has always done, once you give up this benighted notion of trumping your father."

Clay opened his flask and took a swig of brandy. Jerry meant well, but he didn't know how the earl treated his wife. "I cannot give it up," he said softly. "And any marriage is better than the one he plans for me."

"Are you sure?" Bertie wagged a finger at him. "Sounds to me like you're cutting off your nose to smite your face."

"Spite," Jerry said. "To *spite* his face. But you are spot on, Bertie. It is spite that drives him now. Am I right, Clay?"

"To an extent." Clay remembered his wild ride from Montford House to Thurleigh after the confrontation with his father. Had he chanced to encounter a whore or a toothless hag selling rags, he'd have swept her off to London, acquired a special license, and made vows. He had been that angry.

34

Luckily, the roads had been deserted. And a new passion had since replaced his impulse to punish Montford any way he could. "As a matter of fact," he said, "I am *after* rather more than either of you know, and I'll need your help when we get to London. Will you stand with me?"

Bertie swallowed the last of his pie and belched. "Always with you, Clay. We stick together."

Jerry folded his arms. "No one gets hurt?"

Clay looked at him with surprise. That was not a question that ever arose when the three of them began an adventure. "Only the earl, I trust. Surely you cannot object to that. I doubt the Albatross knows of my existence, so she will be unaffected. As for the chaperone, you may safely leave her to me." He chuckled softly. "She has a will of her own, and a strong one at that. If I cannot win her over, so be it."

"You intend to play fair?" Jerry looked doubtful. "We are no longer schoolboys, and females are easily hurt. Their feelings and reputations ought not to be trifled with."

"Do you mean I should not seduce her?" Clay couldn't help but imagine the scene. His gentle, compelling summons. Her retreat. The suggestive words and the sly touches. Her slow, reluctant capitulation. Finally, her eager—

"Are you listening?" Jerry demanded. "Bed her if you must, and if she agrees, but that's no way to begin a marriage."

"I beg to disagree. Half the marriages in England produce children within a few months of the ceremony." Clay swiped his fingers through his hair. "But no, I'll not drag her to the altar because she is increasing. Most likely she will jump at my offer for even more practical reasons—money, a life of leisure, and the chance to escape Bromley Childe's household.

35

Good Lord, she stands to be Countess of Montford one day. How can she possibly turn me down?"

"You have a heart of ice, my friend. I wonder you have not dispatched an accountant to your prospective bride, with a ledger book listing the pros and cons of wedding a disgraced viscount and acquiring a tyrannical father-in-law."

"Only because the cons would far outweigh the benefits. Nevertheless, I shall pursue the governess until she consents to be my wife. A friendly wager, Jerry? Five hundred guineas that I succeed."

Bertie, snoring loudly, had slumped against his brother's shoulder. With a sigh, Jerry pushed him away. "He drinks too much, and I cannot stop him. We need some occupation beyond revelry, Clay. All three of us."

"I did try," Clay reminded him.

"Yes. But your heart wasn't with the army or you'd have found a way to outwit the earl, even if it meant taking the king's shilling. You haven't asked, but I'll tell you what I think. Stop reacting to your father and go in search of what you want for yourself."

Good advice, except that everything he wanted was tangled up with his father. Even Francesca, although he would have wanted her anyway.

But Jerry was right about one thing. She must not be hurt. "Forget the bet," he said. "Neither of us has fifty guineas, let alone five hundred. I'll not begin my courtship of Miss Francesca Nobody by making her the object of a wager."

"A wise decision. Women have a way of finding out about these things. Her name is Francesca? Sounds foreign."

"I suspect she's Italian. Maybe Spanish or Portuguese, but it doesn't matter where she came from. I intend to marry her, and I require your assistance."

"Not for a reference, I trust?"

"Perish the thought. Even without your accounting of my sins, she is convinced I am Satan in a waistcoat. I merely want you and Bertie to draw the Childe girls away, giving me time alone with their chaperone. We saw only the tart in the gaming room, but apparently there are two of them."

"Twins," Jerry said laconically. "I encountered the other one in the taproom when she was looking for her father. Ann. Quiet and shy, nothing like her sister."

Clay regarded his friend with interest. "Something new here?"

"Let us say I am willing to keep her occupied while you make sheep eyes at the dragon. So what is the plan?"

Devil if he knew. "By the time we reach London, I'll have one. Certainly we must be present wherever young girls go to find husbands. Polish up your dancing shoes, Jerry. We may be forced to do the pretty at Almack's."

"Bertie will have to pull off a miracle to get us admitted there. Especially after—" He shrugged. "Well, you know what to expect."

Clay tipped his hat over his eyes and folded his arms, ending the conversation. Yes, he knew precisely what to expect in London. Gossip. Titters behind gloved hands. Pointing fingers. Humiliation.

Francesca was bound to hear of his disgrace, reinforcing her low opinion of Lord Clayburn and making his courtship all the more unwelcome. But failure was out of the question. Within a month he would woo and win his reluctant goddess, rescue his mother, and consign his father to the devil.

The Fates must have a sense of humor, Clay reflected. He had wanted to go to war. And now, in a backward sort of way, he'd got his wish.

Chapter 4

Clere be thy virgyns, lusty underkellis:
London, thou art the flour of Cities all.
                                        —*William Dunbar*

"Such a waste," Francesca said, stepping away from the ballroom door to let a carpenter pass with an armful of wooden moldings. "All this turmoil and expense, just to give a ball."

Maria Beaton brushed sawdust from her skirt. "How tiresome it must be, listening to the ceaseless clatter. And when they begin to paint, the smell of fumes will be positively unendurable. You should consider relocating to the Crillon for a few days, my dear."

"Set Livvy loose in a hotel? Oh, I think not. Although it *would* detach her from the young carpenter she has been hounding for the past two weeks."

"How came you to lease this monstrosity?" Maria asked on their way downstairs. "The location is excellent, to be sure, and the public rooms are in tolerable condition—"

"*Now* they are!" Francesca laughed. "When we arrived, the Holland covers had yet to be removed, and with every step on the carpets, we kicked up a cloud of dust. I'm afraid the owner withheld a few details. He assured our agent that the house was fully staffed but failed to add that the servants were unacquainted with the concept of work. As for the ballroom, he gave only the dimensions. You must admit it is a very *large* ballroom. Regrettably, only mice and spiders have danced there for several decades."

"Deplorable! Someone must answer for this."

"I assure you, someone is. Papa's agent has renegotiated the lease, and now the owner is virtually paying us to stay here."

When they arrived in the foyer, Francesca led her friend down a wide passageway and opened a heavy oak door at the far end. "The library. Notice there are precisely seven volumes on the shelves—the ones I brought with me. Do you suppose we shall have time to visit a bookshop this afternoon?"

"I can always find time for books, my dear. And, of course, we must also see to your wardrobe."

Francesca glanced down at her blue kerseymere walking dress. "But it is already seen to, except for a few items that have not been delivered. Livvy insisted that we set out for the mantua-maker the very day we arrived in London. Indeed, outfitting the three of us is the only task I have managed to complete."

"Perhaps not altogether. That dress is marginally fashionable, but pale colors do not suit you. When we have done with our calls, I shall put you in the capable hands of Madame Flambeau."

Francesca abruptly closed the library door and marched in the direction of the foyer, leaving her guest to follow. How dare Maria Beaton criticize her gown! It was the outside of enough to fall into bed exhausted after wrangling with servants and leasing agents and carpenters and Livvy—always Livvy!— only to toss and turn all the night, fretting over the mountain of tasks still awaiting her attention.

She worried about Papa, whose letters were invariably cheerful so that she would not worry. Which only made her worry all the more.

Bromley rarely came to the house now, after she'd

made it clear the duke had forbidden her to give him so much as a shilling. She was pleased not to have him underfoot, certainly, but his long disappearances made her uneasy. So far as she knew, he had no acquaintances in the city, and even a here-and-thereian required a place to sleep.

After a fortnight in London, she had yet to find time for a visit to the galleries and museums. All her dreams of mingling with people who shared her intellectual interests had been replaced with nightmares about recalcitrant maids, dull-witted cooks, and greedy dressmakers.

Finally, two days ago, she'd stolen an hour to call on the woman with whom she had corresponded for more than a decade. Maria Beaton, noted bluestocking and advocate of women's rights, had always encouraged her meager pretensions to learning. Francesca often spent hours, sometimes days, researching and drafting her replies to Maria's letters.

Now she understood what a trial it must have been for Maria to indulge the Rutlandshire yokel. Even this brief time in London had proven she lacked the experience and sophistication to deal with simple tradesmen, let alone with the beau monde.

Francesca realized she had come to a stop in the foyer, with her hand clutching a carved newel for support.

Maria tapped her briskly on the shoulder. "Are you done with the fidgets, young woman? We must be on our way."

"I cannot go with you." Francesca tightened her grip on the newel. "I simply cannot."

"Nonsense. Stand up straight, turn yourself around, and look at me."

Fairly sure Bonaparte would obey an order delivered in that tone of voice, Francesca straightened and turned. With effort, she looked directly into Maria's calm brown eyes.

"I haven't the merest idea how to go on in Society," she confessed, relieved to say out loud what she had been thinking since Papa first proposed this scheme. "They will laugh at me, all the hoity-toity ladies you mean for me to meet today. Not while I am in their company, certainly, for they are far too well mannered. But afterward, I shall be talked about like a two-headed pig at the county fair."

"Only if you oink, my dear. And should you do so, it may well start a fashion for oinking. Recollect that you are the daughter of a duke."

"Only the adopted daughter. And I'm half-Italian, by birth an illegitimate commoner. Also a country bumpkin."

"And thereby all the more fascinating." When Francesca began to object, Maria waved a hand dismissively. "Needless to say, we shall never discuss the circumstances of your birth. Sotherton accepted you, and that is all anyone needs to know. Moreover, you must recall that *I* am sponsoring you. A mixed blessing, what with a few doors closed to me, but the stiff-backed snobs behind them are of no account. I expect you to become the Toast of the Season."

"And I expect the high sticklers will have me for toast."

"Oh, Lud, do postpone this attack of megrims until a later time. We are expected at Lady Softon's within the half hour. Where is your wrap, child? My horses have been kept waiting too long as it is." Maria clapped her hands. "Hop to it!"

Francesca practically leaped for the bell-rope.

After several minutes, Maria pacing restlessly all the while, the sour-faced butler shuffled into the foyer, still pulling on his coat.

Maria examined him with searing displeasure. "Watch and learn, my dear," she murmured to Francesca before advancing on the butler with the force of a bullet. "Miss Childe has just informed me that you are to be dismissed. What is your name?"

"P-Peters, ma'am." He took a quick step back, and then another, until Maria had forced him to the wall.

"I have asked that she reconsider, Peters. But henceforth you are on trial, as is each and every servant in the household. Miss Childe naturally expected a period of adjustment, but her patience has now run out. Do we understand each other?"

"Yes, ma'am. Completely."

Maria moved aside, allowing him room to bow to Francesca. "What do you wish, Miss Childe?" he asked with amazing deference. "I am at your service."

Torn between awe and a fit of the giggles, Francesca lifted her chin. "Have the maid fetch down my pelisse, bonnet, gloves, and reticule. Also an umbrella. Send a footman to inform Mrs. Beaton's driver that we are on our way out. And I rely on you, Peters, to make sure Miss Olivia does not leave this house while I am gone."

As the butler hurried off, Francesca turned to Maria. "How was that?"

"A good beginning, my dear. Next time be more haughty, as if you expect a task to be done before you think to order it. Servants in a leased house have not a grain of loyalty, and they will be just as lazy and insolent as you permit."

The peevish lady's maid Francesca had inherited with the other servants, bony arms full of a woolen fur-collared pelisse, bonnet, and gloves, was nearly trampled as Livvy charged down the staircase directly behind her.

"Where are you going, Cesca?" Livvy demanded, shoving the maid aside. "I want to go with you."

"Not today," Francesca said, aware of Maria watching her attentively. Servants were not the only recalcitrant dependents she must learn to handle. "Have you forgot, Livvy? There is to be another dancing lesson at one o'clock."

"Pah! Monsieur barely manages to waddle through the steps, and his stays creak so that I can scarce hear the music. If I must have a teacher, can we not find one who is young and slim and tall?"

Francesca slipped into her pelisse. "Sadly, all the desirable dance masters have already run off with silly girls. You must settle for Monsieur Peltier and his wife, who plays the pianoforte well, don't you think? And while we are on the subject of wives, the carpenter you've been tormenting has one of his own. Let him alone, Livvy."

"Oh, very well." She nibbled her lip. "He's told me the same thing. But I'm *bored*, Cesca. You cannot close me up in this mausoleum for the rest of my life!"

The image of Livvy laid out on a marble slab, silenced forever, made Francesca's fingers curl. Sometimes she truly longed to strangle the girl. "Today Mrs. Beaton ... the same Mrs. Beaton you have so rudely ignored ... will present me to five fashionable ladies. And we are paying these calls for the sole purpose of securing invitations to their routs and balls. For *you*, Livvy. And Ann, of course. I personally have no interest in balls and routs. What is more, you will be barred from every door unless you deport yourself like a gently bred young lady. Do you understand?"

"Yes, Francesca." She made her curtsy to Maria. "Pleased to meet you, Mrs. Beaton. Forgive my poor manners. I have lived all my life in the country and am still learning how to go on."

From the militant gleam in her eyes, Francesca

knew Livvy had learned nothing at all, except when to cut her losses and beat a retreat.

It was a relief to be settled in Maria's carriage a few minutes later, even though they were on their way to meet the crème de la crème of London Society. "You must think me a self-pitying, whiny ninny-hammer," Francesca said by way of apology. "Truly, in the general way I am nothing of the sort. My faults run more toward a flashpan temper and a lamentable tendency to act without thought."

"I have noticed," Maria said dryly. "Had you stopped a moment to consider in the last few weeks, you would have sought help instead of shouldering every burden alone."

"Add pride to my list of flaws. I find it difficult to ask for assistance and often refuse help when it is freely offered. Ludicrous, is it not, since I am the veriest child of charity? If not for Papa's benevolence, I would be scrounging an existence on the streets of Naples. More likely, I would be dead."

"And now you are determined to prove that you can make your way unassisted. Perfectly understandable. As a champion of female independence, I hesitate to dissuade you." Maria smiled. "But we all require help to achieve our goals, and we help others in return, to keep the river flowing. Ask and give, Francesca. That is my lesson for today. Now compose yourself, for here is our first stop."

Two hours and five calls later, Francesca emerged from Lady Jersey's mansion with the promise of vouchers to Almack's ringing in her ears. The wind promptly upturned her umbrella, but even the cold rain pelting her bonnet and pelisse could not dampen her excitement.

"We did it!" she exclaimed as the footman closed the carriage door. "Maria, you are a treasure. How did you manage to bring me through this ordeal? I was absolutely terrified at each and every visit. And when that cucumber slice flew out of my sandwich and onto Lady Jersey's lap, I just knew that I was ruined forever. Whatever did you say to make her laugh? I was so busy trying not to faint that I failed to hear you."

Maria placidly adjusted her sable-lined cloak. "Nor have you heard the last of that cucumber. She will enjoy recounting the tale, as I quickly pointed out."

"Oh dear."

" 'Tis nothing to worry about. In fact, providing Sally that tidbit of gossip was your greatest accomplishment. Now she will be your staunchest ally, and see to it that you and the twins are welcomed everywhere."

A lump settled in Francesca's throat. "How can I ever thank you, Maria? Or repay you?"

"Pish-posh! As a rule, I find London Society tedious. But I need to preserve my influence with these people, and you give me a delightful excuse to set aside my books and lectures for a few weeks. Shall we agree to be mutually indebted?"

Only if I can keep Livvy from shaming us both, Francesca thought. She glanced up at Maria, who was regarding her with concern. "Mutually? No. I absolutely reserve the right to be indebted. Shall we go to the bookshop now?"

"Oh no, young woman." Maria's expression grew stern. "First I mean to hand you over to Madame Flambeau. Unlike your former mantua-maker, who dressed you like the pale English beauty you are not, she will fit you in the simple styles and vibrant colors that suit you."

"But what does it matter how I look? I shall attend balls only to chaperone Ann and Livvy."

"If you wish to repay me for introducing you to the

ton," Maria said firmly, "begin by making me proud of your appearance. Madame is a most annoying woman, as you will soon discover, but Hatchard's Book Shop will be your reward for patience."

Chapter 5

He is stark mad, whoever says
That he has been in love an hour.
                                      —*John Donne*

It was a typical winter afternoon at White's, with fires crackling at each end of the reading room, the occasional rustle of newspapers, and the low rumble of male voices. Slumped on a wing-back chair in one corner, Sir Harvey Felterpell snored in rhythm with the rain beating against the windows.

Clay passed a coin to the young footman who had remembered to keep his coffee cup filled for the past two hours. "Any luck yet?"

"I checked all the rooms again, milord, but they have not come in." He added a log to the fire. "The doorman will direct them here when they arrive."

Alone again, Clay stretched his legs toward the hearth and stared moodily into the flames. He'd always considered patience his chief virtue, and he carefully nurtured his supply because a gamester who made his living at the tables required a great deal of it.

But the past two weeks would have tried the endurance of a saint. As gossip about his aborted army commission swirled around him, he could do little but grip the edges of his dignity and hang on. At the clubs and other haunts of fashionable gentlemen, he replied to lifted brows and sly gibes from his fellows with careless humor. The young men could scarcely accuse him of cowardice, after all, since not a one of them was off fighting Napoleon either. And the older men, who knew the Earl of Montford and the power he wielded, had some degree of sympathy for his besieged son.

But Clay knew the worst was yet to come. He had received no invitations, not even from hostesses who generally welcomed a titled rake. Not that he would give a twig, in the usual course of things, since balls, routs, and musicales bored him senseless. But those were the sorts of places at which Francesca would be found, so he must contrive to be there, too.

He sipped at his coffee, mentally lining up targets. Sally Jersey would surely restore him to her list, if he offered up a morsel of tittle-tattle about the scandal, and her rivals would jump just as eagerly to the bait. The idea of approaching them hat in hand made his stomach turn, but it might well come to that. Jerry and Bertie had dutifully made an appearance at all the important pre-Season parties without catching a glimpse of his quarry.

It seemed that Francesca, along with Bromley Childe and his twin vixens, had gone to ground somewhere in London. Or returned from whence they had come, wherever that was. How little he knew of the woman he planned to marry! More peculiar still, he could practically feel her in his arms whenever he thought about her, which was most of the time.

Everything in him that was male had sprung to attention the first time he'd seen her. But he'd also divined any number of logical reasons to woo and wed the beautiful Francesca. She was a woman of inconsequential birth and questionable breeding, which served his purposes exactly. When presented with his new daughter-in-law, Montford would understand immediately what she represented—a final avowal of independence by his son. Moreover, once she gave him a child, he could secure the inheritance from his grandmother and provide a new home for his mother.

Rational, perfectly acceptable reasons to find and marry the elusive goddess. He could almost believe them himself.

But where his reason stopped and the rest of him began, he was utterly obsessed with her.

"Pardon me if I am de trop," a voice said near his shoulder. "I'll take m'self off if you prefer. Or maybe you don't remember me at all. Most people don't."

Startled, Clay looked up at the round, pleasant face of Lord Mumblethorpe. He was in no mood for company, but good manners forced him to his feet. "A pleasure to see you again, Mumblethorpe. Etonians always remember their schoolfellows."

"The Brotherhood," Mumblethorpe said. "More in theory than in fact, but you were kind when I followed you about like a puppy the whole first term. Certainly I shall not repay you by intruding on your privacy yet again. Thing is, I am just returned from paying a call on Lady Sefton. Your name came up in the conversation."

"Unsurprising, since my latest fall from grace is on everyone's lips."

"For the moment." Obviously nervous, Mumblethorpe cleared his throat. "Once the Season is in full swing, new gossip will replace this rather dull tale. No offense, but the buying and selling of a military commission is of little concern to those who dance and make merry while England is at war. Should you choose to create a genuine scandal, preferably involving a woman or a duel, we shall all happily natter about it over tea and cakes." He flushed from his neckcloth to his receding hairline. "Fact is, some of us never do anything of note, so we busy ourselves passing judgment on the people we envy."

Clay was astonished to think of anyone envying him. What had he ever accomplished, beyond surviving a virulent hangover or winning enough at the gaming tables to pay off his creditors? On the whole, he had lived a remarkably useless life.

"Well, I don't mean to make a nuisance of m'self," Mumblethorpe said when Clay failed to speak. "Thing is, Lady Sefton asked me if she ought to send you an invitation, and I put her off because I didn't know what to say. Her ball will be the first of significance since Parliament convened, but perhaps you do not wish to appear in Society. Under the circumstances, that is. Thought I'd ask you, before I gave her an answer."

His words faded off at the end, to the point where Clay barely heard them. A shy man, Clay thought. With his plain looks and timid manners, Mumblethorpe probably drew as little attention now as he had done at Eton. "You think she'll send me a card on your say-so?"

Mumblethorpe gave a diffident shrug. "Perhaps. She is unaccountably fond of me."

"Then I applaud her taste. And if she is kind enough to admit me, I shall attend the ball with great pleasure. You may assure her that I'll behave myself."

Mumblethorpe accepted Clay's extended hand with a surprisingly strong grip. "As to that, she may well prefer that you do not. The whole point of giving a ball is to have everyone talk about it for weeks. I'll be off now. Good to see you again, Clayburn."

Bemused, Clay resettled on his chair. How odd that a youngster he'd scarcely acknowledged at Eton had resurfaced just in time to do him a favor. To be sure, there was no certainty Lady Sefton's invitation would materialize, but it didn't signify. He liked Mumblethorpe. One day, when Lord Clayburn was a respectably married pattern card of propriety, perhaps they could be friends.

"There you are!" Jerry clapped him on the shoulder. "Thought for sure you'd be tossing dice. The doorman tried to lead us here, but we had to poke our noses in the gaming room first."

"I am a reformed man," Clay advised him cordially.

"Don't look it." Bertie tugged a chair closer to the fire. "Missed a spot by the ear when you shaved. Bloodshot eyes. Disposition like a bear."

"Devil it, I've spent the last fortnight prowling through every gaming hell in London. What do you expect?"

"You've spent half your life in those very same hells," Jerry pointed out. "Never bothered you before. So, any word of Bromley Childe?"

"Nothing of use. Last night I found one man who remembered him from a club in Manchester and another who once tossed dice with him in York. From what I can tell, this may be his first trip to London. Who knows where he'll turn up?"

"Bad luck, that, what with gamesters being easier to root out than obscure young ladies from the provinces." Jerry propped an arm on the mantelpiece. "No sign of the chits so far, although we've spent all week paying calls on the tabbies. Even went to a musicale last night. Bertie was evicted for snoring. It would be a lot easier, y'know, if we could ask a few direct questions."

"Well, you cannot." Clay rubbed his forehead. "I won't compromise their reputations before they have even made their come-out. Francesca would never forgive me."

"Can't matter," Bertie observed, "if you don't ever see her again."

51

"Oh, I'll find her." Clay drained the last of the coffee from his cup. "And it's just occurred to me how to go about it. Why did I fail to think of this earlier? The Tongue will know."

"The Tongue knows everything," Bertie said reverently.

"But I thought she was dead," Jerry put in. "Wasn't there a funeral? Everybody went but me. I had a cold."

"The corpse was her last husband. Or maybe not her last. She may have remarried by now." Clay grimaced. "She'll ring a peal over me for neglecting to call, and another for popping in uninvited today. Want to come along?"

"Not me!" Jerry and Bertie replied in unison.

Clay stood and bowed. "I am in your debt, gentlemen, and forgive me for wasting your time to no purpose. The Tongue will have the answers we've all been looking for."

He was waiting in the foyer for his coat, hat, and gloves when the door swung open, a blast of cold air preceding two grumbling men who had apparently been caught in the rainstorm.

Without pleasure, Clay recognized Lord Rupert Heston and Clarence Briggs, a pair of weasels who had set out to make his life miserable from the day he first set foot at Eton. It was tradition for the older boys to persecute newcomers, of course, but Heston had taken a personal, inexplicable dislike to the eight-year-old viscount, one that had grown stronger over the years. Briggs, without a single opinion to call his own, followed Heston like a shadow and echoed his every word.

True to form, Heston no sooner spotted his old adversary than he raised the sword. "I say, Clayburn, why lurk you here in the foyer? Taken employment as a footman?" He removed his wet curly-brimmed beaver and held it out. "Make sure to brush this carefully."

"Here's m'gloves," Briggs said, tossing them in Clay's direction.

Clay ignored Heston's hat and the gloves that landed at his feet, but he was very much aware of the men gathering in the passageway, sniffing a quarrel like hounds on the scent.

Heston's lips narrowed. Whipcord-lean and graceful in the manner of an experienced fencer, he always relished an audience for the scenes he created. This one, Clay knew from the glint in his mocking eyes, would be particularly ugly.

"Snap to it!" Heston ordered when Clay failed to acknowledge him. "My hat requires cleaning. Should you fail to do your duty, I shall complain to the management and have you turned off." He added maliciously, "How then will you earn your bread . . . since the army won't have you?"

"He don't even qualify as a mess sergeant," Briggs chimed in, preening when a few onlookers chuckled. "Good thing the likes of him ain't standing between England and Bonaparte. We'd all wind up speaking Frenchie."

"Not you," Clay said to Briggs with a smile. "You have yet to master English."

When that quiet observation elicited a smattering of applause, Briggs sidled into a corner, leaving Clay and Heston to confront each other directly. The small space where they stood was charged with mutual antagonism.

Clay, with the impassive expression of a gambler holding bad cards, waited for Heston to make the next play.

"Where's your papa?" Heston inquired silkily. "I had thought he always kept close by, to hold your leading strings. But after buying back your army commission and making you the laughingstock of

53

London, he seems to have vaporized. How unfortunate. Who will protect you now, I wonder?"

Clay examined Heston slowly from boots to scalp. "Protect me from what?"

He shrugged dramatically. "The rain? Who can tell what will spook a coward?"

The audience sucked in a collective breath.

Coward. The word had been said, to his face and in front of witnesses. "Not you," Clay said with a quelling look. "Rupert Heston couldn't spook a kitten. But if you are of a mind to fight, sir, I am more than ready to oblige you."

"Are you calling me out then?"

"If you require a challenge, I might consider producing one. But then, a formal duel would mean rising at dawn, which neither of us has done in recent memory. Not to mention appointing seconds who are honor-bound to negotiate a peaceful settlement if one is to be had." He gestured to Clarence Briggs. "Do you really want that nincompoop speaking on your behalf? I believe he is your only friend."

"I can negotiate for myself," Heston snarled. "Name your weapon!"

"Ah, I seem to have misunderstood. You are calling *me* out. Very well, then, but I'll not give you the advantage by choosing swords. A bullet between your eyes will save us both a great deal of time. Assuming I have correctly interpreted the situation, of course. Precisely who is challenging whom?"

Laughter erupted from the bystanders, and during the brief lapse of tension, the servant holding Clay's incidentals managed to shoulder through the crowd.

Not altogether pleased at the interruption, Clay took his greatcoat and pulled it on, watching Heston closely. After two weeks of public humiliation, he was spoiling for a fight, and who better to exterminate than the man he had loathed for twenty years. Hell, if not for Francesca, he would long since have picked up one of Briggs's gloves and slapped it in Heston's face.

To his disappointment, Heston backed off with a languid wave of his hand. "If Montford will not permit his son to fight Bonaparte, I daresay he'd throw himself between the two of us if we came to blows. To spare an old man the trouble, and for that reason only, I bid you good day."

"Thank heavens for that. I had thought you meant to bore me to death." Clay drew on his gloves, set his hat on his head, and nodded to the footman, who hurried to open the door.

Spikes of wind-driven rain pounded his face as he slogged through ankle-deep puddles toward Pall Mall, where hacks were lined up waiting to be hired. He climbed into the first coach after shouting Eudora's address several times to the jarvey, who wore a heavy set of earmuffs against the cold.

Clay settled on the lumpy squabs and folded his arms. Just as well it had come to nothing, he supposed. A duel would have forced him to leave England for a year or two, and that was no longer possible.

He had to find Francesca.

Chapter 6

Why should we defer our joys?
Fame and rumor are but toys.
                                        —*Ben Jonson*

"Well, well. Long past time you deigned to call, rascal!"

Clay gave Lady Eudora Swann the flamboyant, old-fashioned bow she expected. "Your servant, ma'am."

She snorted. "Oh, Lud, you sweet-talking men! Vows of servitude at every turn, with not the least intention of following through. Where are you, Felicia? Push me into the light, gel."

While Eudora's ancient companion shuffled to her feet and guided her employer's Bath chair to the center of the room, Clay smiled fondly at the most intriguing creature he had ever known.

She had changed little since last year. Sleek ebony hair, dyed with boot-blacking, he suspected, formed a helmet over her wrinkled, rice-powdered face. Her thin lips were stained berry-red, as were her cheekbones and, probably, her nipples. But for all the flamboyant jewelry and garish cosmetics, it was her pair of canny blue eyes that held his attention.

At four-and-eighty, Eudora retained her sharp wits and even sharper tongue. She had married and buried five or six husbands that he knew of, including two earls and a viscount, but now she played the game of love for vicarious amusement. Or so he assumed. For all he really knew, she had a lover waiting upstairs in her bedchamber. He rather hoped she did.

"Come closer, boy," she commanded, raising her lorgnette. "Sit here on the divan where I can see you. Closer. No, closer than that. Open the curtains, Felicia. Cast some light on this devilish handsome lordling."

Clay blinked as daylight flooded into the stuffy room. "You are the true beauty, my dear."

"And you are in trouble again," she shot back. "I am so glad of it. These last few weeks have been prodigiously dull. Felicia, ring for tea. No, go below-stairs and bring it up yourself. But be slow about it, for I wish to be private with Clayburn."

"Not proper," Felicia muttered as she shambled to the door. "Not proper."

"These old women!" Eudora put a gnarled hand on Clay's thigh. "No heart under their saggy breasts. They die to life so long before they're planted in the ground."

"While you remain ever young," Clay replied, sincerely. "If I should make an offer, Lady Grace, would you marry me?"

"In a heartbeat, sir." She slid her fingers up his leg. "Are you asking?"

"Ah, left to my own devices, I would happily do so. But there remains the pernicious matter of siring an heir."

"Titles do come equipped with obligations," she agreed with a disappointed sigh "And for all the considerable prowess of my several husbands, I never managed to pop out a babe. No reason to expect that will change now."

"A pity," Clay said. "The world would be richer with your children in it."

"More interesting, certainly." Her wandering fingers moved closer to his privates. "Consider this.

Once you are wed and have got a son on your wife, you will require a mistress." She grinned over pointy yellow teeth. "I'd not turn you away, Clayburn."

Just before her fingertips reached their target, he slipped a hand gently under her wrist and lifted it for a kiss. "I am rehearsing fidelity, my sweet. And as that is scarcely a role I am accustomed to, I must implore you not to tempt me beyond my strength."

"Fidelity? *You?*" She sat back in her chair, clearly astounded.

The very idea of it amazed him, too, and he could hardly explain to her what he did not understand. For the moment he put the astounding notion aside. He had more pressing business to attend to. "While I am naturally delighted to see you again," he said, "I have, in fact, come to you for information."

"Most everyone does, sooner or later. But you know the rules, Clayburn. Tit for tat. No offense, but I must take in more gossip than I give out, or I'll soon run dry." She folded her arms. "You may proceed."

"Let me see. Recently I bought a commission in the army, whereupon my father pulled strings to seize it back without consulting me."

"Stale news. I heard this paltry tale weeks ago. Montford intrigues me, self-righteous looby that he is, and I am up on his every move. Do you know, I expect I am better acquainted with his enterprises than you are."

"Almost certainly. He is of no concern whatever to me, until he interferes with my life. And apparently his latest attempt to meddle will not buy me so much as the answer to a question."

"True enough," Eudora said without mercy. "You'll have to do better."

Clay loosened his neckcloth. "This you cannot possibly have heard, as it occurred less than an hour ago. Lord Heston made an ass of himself at White's, and I almost called him out."

"Almost? I give you no credit for *almost*, Clayburn. Someone should have put a bullet between his eyes long since. In my experience, his transgressions are seldom of any consequence. Worse, they are never amusing."

Laughing, Clay stood and crossed to the window overlooking Upper Brook Street. "Alas, poor Eudora. The only gossip I can place on your altar relates to a tedious villain and a reformed rake."

"Reformed!" She wheeled in his direction so quickly that he had to grab the chair before she propelled herself through the window glass. "Tell me more."

"Got your attention, did I?" He squeezed her thin shoulder with affection. "Perhaps this will loose your tongue. I am soon to be married."

The stunned silence following that pronouncement gave him enormous satisfaction, and enough time to regret what he had just disclosed. "Please understand this information is for your ears only," he added hastily. "Until I inform the bride of my intentions—"

"Who is she?" Eudora demanded.

"Have I your word to keep the secret until I release you?"

"Yes, yes. Excluding hints. Do not forbid me a few hints."

He dropped to one knee beside her chair and gazed directly into her eyes. "You'll say nothing to the point, Eudora. I need your help and will beg for it if need be. But I won't have the woman I mean to wed become the object of speculation and scandal."

Eudora chewed on her lower lip. "Oh, very well, you irritating boy."

"Thank you." He brushed his lips across her papery

cheek. "Now tell me everything you know about Francesca Childe."

"Never heard of her. Wait. Childe. The name is familiar."

Clay lowered his other knee, leaning both hands against Eudora's chair as she closed her eyes. She was casting back, he knew, through her remarkable store of memories. Eudora Swann was a veritable repository of the past, the song-singer of nearly a century of aristocratic history. Like Homer, she could recount whole epics about the lords and ladies who had caught her interest, and most did.

She emerged from her recollections with a start. "Ah yes, I have it now. Melchior Childe. The Duke of Sotherton. 'Lord Least-in-Sight,' we called him in the old days. But he's not set foot in London since the Great Scandal. How came you to know him?"

"I don't," he said, wondering if the Great Scandal involved Francesca. "More to the point, what do *you* know of him?"

Eudora tapped her fingers on the arm of her chair. "Little enough, I fear. He married Lord Glenchester's youngest, a sweet-faced, vapid chit who died shortly after. He fled to the Continent then, and no more was heard of him for several years. But all this took place before you were born. Why should you care— Oh!" She prodded Clay on the chest. "What a slowpoke I am! You must be sniffing after the mysterious daughter. Am I right? If Montford gets wind of this, he will chain you in the attics."

"I'll deal with my father when the time comes," Clay said evenly. "Tell me about the daughter. And the scandal."

" 'Twas most savory, while it lasted. All the hopeful mamas were longing for Sotherton's return, rich eligible dukes being thin on the ground. Then word came he had married abroad and resettled on his estate with an Italian wife of dubious lineage. Renalda was her name, as I recall. She had a child, possibly by a previous marriage. Nobody knows for certain. Sotherton immediately set his lawyers to arrange an adoption, so the child cannot have been his own."

Eudora frowned. "Someone, probably one of the disappointed mamas, took to calling this negligible business the Great Scandal. But as Sotherton never again appeared in Society, there were no fresh rumors to fan the fires and they soon died down. Nothing more was heard of him until a decade ago, when notice of his wife's death appeared in the *Times*."

Clay stood and brushed carpet lint from his breeches. "He must not have had a son by his Italian wife, because I understand his brother is to inherit the title. Lord Bromley Childe."

"A flea-wit if ever there was one! Last I heard, he was staging cockfights in Yorkshire. So he has come to London, you say? Here to fire off the twins, no doubt, but I'd thought him pockets-to-let. How is he to finance their come-out?"

"Perhaps His Grace is paying for it. Sotherton's daughter has come along as chaperone, or did you already know?"

Eudora picked at her shawl. "As I cannot leave this house without considerable difficulty, I must wait for news to come to me. And Bromley Childe is of less significance than a climbing boy. Who would think to mention him or his whelps?"

Clay grinned. "Your reputation stands, my sweet. If not for a chance encounter at a posthouse, I would not be aware of their existence either. Nor would I have met the duke's mysterious daughter."

"So we arrive at the point," Eudora said slyly. "Francesca. The bride who does not yet know of your intention to marry her. What exactly happened at that posthouse, wicked man? Did you seduce her?"

"Lord, no. Well, under the circumstances, I could not. Miss Childe and I spent no more than a few minutes together, never privately."

Eudora clapped her hands. "How delicious! It was the same with me and my second husband. No, my third. I forget precisely which man was involved, but the *feeling* was unmistakable. Love at first sight, yes?"

"No indeed, you atrocious wench. For my part, it was sheer lust at first sight. And as for her reaction to me—"

He rubbed the back of his neck, which grew tight as he recalled their first meeting. "Truth be told, she took me into immediate dislike. *Loathing* is probably a more accurate term. But I must add that she did not see me at my best."

"Drinking and gaming, were you? I daresay she could come across you doing the same at any time or place." Eudora wheeled closer to where he stood, her eyes alight with curiosity. "Why do you want the foreign girl, Clayburn? Lust soon flames out, leaving ashes and heartbreak. Believe me on this point, for I know all there is to know about lust. Or is it the money? Sotherton may will his considerable fortune to his brother, you know."

She nudged the wheel of her chair against his leg. "Never tell me you mean to punish your father by marrying a wife he cannot approve? Montford is too much the snob to accept a woman of mixed ancestry."

"It is fortunate, then, that he will not be the one taking her to wife. As for the Sotherton inheritance, I care not if Francesca comes to me barefoot and in rags."

Eudora patted him on the backside. "Excellent. There is hope for you yet. But I wish to take the girl's measure, Clayburn. You must bring her here as soon as may be."

"Gladly. But first I must find her again. Like 'Lord Least-in-Sight,' she has a knack for disappearing." He went to the secretaire and wrote his address on the back of a calling card. "Should anything more about the duke and his family come to mind, please send word."

Eudora accepted the card and slid it down the lacy bodice of her gown. "Sotherton was ever a bookish fellow," she reflected. "Even in his youth he haunted the auction houses, buying collections for his library. Seems to me he was especially fond of poetry."

"You think she inherited a taste for literature?" he asked, welcoming any clue that might lead him to Francesca's heart, if not her location.

"Well, how could she inherit anything at all, being another man's daughter? But he doubtless encouraged her to share his interests, and what else is there to do in the wild northlands but read?" She chuckled. "Or have a tumble with a well-hung farmhand. That would certainly be my choice."

Clay dropped onto a chair. "By the stars, Eudora, compared to you I am the veriest choirboy. But since I have called on your memories, may I now draw upon your experience? Once she is found, how am I to proceed with Miss Stiff-and-Proper Childe?"

Through her lorgnette, Eudora ran an intent blue-eyed gaze from the crown of his head to the toes of his Hessian boots. "Find a way to be alone with her," she said tartly. "Then remove your clothes."

"I beg your pardon?"

"That would turn the trick with any woman of spirit. Never mind that I've been unable to walk these last three years. If you stripped to your skin here and now, I'd be out of my chair and on top of you in the blink of an eye. Or under you, if you preferred."

He doubled over with laughter.

" 'Tis no joke, Clayburn. By the grace of God you are a splendid-looking man, and charming to boot. Play to your strengths. Besides, if Miss Childe fails to appreciate your magnificent body, what is the hope for your future together? You cannot mean to spend your life with a cold bedmate." Her eyes narrowed. "Especially if you intend to remain faithful."

He sobered instantly. "I do. Not by choice, you understand. But likely she will demand it."

"She has Italian blood," Eudora reminded him. "Beneath the starchy propriety that holds you at bay, she is Mediterranean sun and drizzles of olive oil over ripe peppers. Never forget that. Nick away at her defenses with proper British wooing and you'll make no progress whatever. But assault her with passion, and she is yours. And if she isn't, you didn't want her anyway!"

"I expect this wooing to be a bit more complicated," he said thoughtfully. "Francesca is something out of the ordinary. And remember, she already detests me. I made a lamentable first impression."

Just then, Felicia staggered into the room, listing from side to side under the shifting weight of crockery and food atop an enormous silver tray. Clay jumped up to take the tray from her hands before she collapsed.

"Very good, Felicia," Eudora said. "Now disappear again until I call for you, and turn away all visitors. It seems that Lord Clayburn requires an education."

Cheeks burning, Clay poured the tea and set thin ham sandwiches and an Eccles cake on a plate for his hostess.

"Are you prepared to heed my advice?" Eudora asked sharply. "As you are unwilling to take the direct approach, and stand convinced that the lady will not be moved by it, let us consider the alternatives."

"By all means," he said numbly.

"When next you meet, you will naturally be the perfect gentleman, to counter the impression she has already formed. At the same time, you must be relentless and romantic. A delicate balance, to be sure, but a woman needs to know that she is desired. The combination of restraint and determination will wear her down."

"Relentless," he said. "Romantic. Restrained."

"Precisely. But meantime, you must prepare for the second phase of this campaign. You will not like it," she warned. "This is the most difficult stage of all. It resides, for Francesca, between mild attraction and sleepless nights."

Whatever that means, Clay thought. Women were damnably complex creatures. "I shall do whatever you say, Eudora."

"I can only wish," she said with a saucy grin that subtracted fifty years from her age. "In any case, you must write her a love poem."

"Bloody hell!"

"It will be, I expect, unless you have a talent for composing verse. But consider. She has only to look at you to know that women leap into your bed if you so much as point the way. As a consequence, you must exert effort to prove that she is extraordinary and that your intentions are sincere."

"So I'll send flowers. Lots of them."

"A trifling matter of passing coins to a flower seller." Eudora wagged a scolding finger. "Pathetic, Clayburn! And could you afford to drape her head to toe in diamonds, which I very much doubt, she would conclude that you wished to set her up as a mistress. Only a poem will do it, lad. Not the careless words a rake uses to bait his hook, but words from your heart."

"Why can't I just write her a letter?" he asked desperately.

"Oh, far too easy. Your avowal of love must present itself in rhyme and meter, however excruciating the process, because she is so very different from all the other women you've wanted and bedded before meeting her."

"She is," he affirmed softly. "But it would be a far sight easier to slay her a dragon than cobble a couplet, let alone an entire poem."

"And she will know it! You begin, at last, to get the point of this exercise. Mind you, stand ready to slay any dragon that crosses her path, and be alert to any favor you can do her, however insignificant. Preferably before she asks. In my experience, men require a kick on the arse to notice when a woman stands in need of help. You must do better."

The Tongue lectured him for another hour before sending him on his way, mildly befuddled and certain only that he had first to write a pestilential poem. God help him. Her other advice would apply only after the wedding, and his ear tips burned to imagine the things Eudora suggested he do with Francesca.

Until this afternoon, he had thought himself an imaginative, considerate lover, but females apparently had a whole different perspective on lovemaking. He was relieved to know that he served up the main course to advantage, but mortified to learn that women were equally partial to the hors d'oeuvres and the dessert.

Well, first things first. He actually liked poetry, so long as it came equipped with a story like the *Odyssey* or "The Rime of the Ancient Mariner." Lyrical jabbering bored him senseless. But if he was going to write a love poem, he probably ought to read a few for inspiration.

The rain had let up, he saw when he reached the street, and luckily, a hackney came by at the same moment. "Hatchard's," he told the driver.

Chapter 7

Lost is our freedom,
When we submit to women so.
— *Thomas Campion*

When the bow windows of Hatchard's came into view, Francesca's weariness vanished straightaway. Books!

The driving rain had stopped sometime during her long ordeal with Madame Flambeau, where she had been measured for gowns no decent woman ought to wear in public. It was the style, Madame insisted, to expose a great deal of bosom. And Francesca had lots of it.

Not that she was pleased to be so lavishly endowed. In her opinion, breasts served no purpose whatever for a female who did not mean to marry and nurse babies. They only got in the way and bounced when she was walking. But there they were, a legacy from her voluptuous mother, and Madame Flambeau had decreed they must be displayed to all and sundry.

Men were partial to women's breasts, Maria explained patiently. They enjoyed looking at them. But what had any of that to do with a woman of one-and-thirty, long past the age to attract a suitor even if she happened to want one? And since she did not, why dress herself to be ogled?

Another of London Society's vast mysteries, she thought as a footman opened the carriage door and lowered the steps.

Walking into the large, well-appointed bookshop felt very much like coming home. To her nostrils, the smell of leather bindings and glue was sweeter than any perfume, and she took a deep, happy breath of musty air.

The shop was crowded with patrons, most busier socializing than buying books. On chairs drawn up to the large fireplace, several men and women leafed through newspapers and periodicals, while clerks wearing aprons moved silently through the lines of standing shelves, locating books the shoppers had requested.

"I see a few people I wish to greet," Maria said, "but you have made enough new acquaintances for one day. Wander about as long as you like, my dear."

"Don't speak too soon," Francesca warned. "When surrounded by books, I generally forget that time exists."

"As do I." Maria gave her a warm smile. "Do you wish directions to particular sorts of—? No, of course not. You'd rather discover them for yourself. Off with you, then."

Francesca headed immediately for the back of the shop, which was all but deserted, and spent a desultory half hour in paradise. Rather than carry the many books she wanted to purchase, she marked their location and took with her only Miss Sydney Owens's new historical novel for fear someone else would snatch the only copy.

"May I disturb you for a moment, Francesca?"

She looked up to see Maria standing a few yards away, in an open space between two blocks of shelves. Beside her was a quietly dressed, somber-looking man about forty years old. He bowed politely when she joined them.

"Francesca, this is Mr. Hatchard, my friend of many

years. John, Miss Childe is likely to be your very best customer while she remains in London, even though you come to her with bad news. Perhaps you should tell her what you have just told me."

His cheeks reddened slightly, but his voice was calm and to the point. "I am pleased to make your acquaintance, ma'am. My news relates to the collection of Petrarch's sonnets you wish to acquire. At one time, I thought we had found it. A book matching your description turned up on a list of items to be auctioned at Christie's, pending valuation."

He glanced at Maria, who gestured for him to proceed. "This morning I learned that the auction has been canceled. That comes as little surprise, to be sure, since the Marquess of Fallon is nothing if not unreliable."

"I'm not sure I understand," Francesca said. "The marquess is the owner of the book, and he has decided to keep it for himself?"

"Not precisely. When the representative of Christie's went to examine the lot up for sale, half the heirlooms on the preliminary list were missing. According to his report, they may well be in the house, which is enormous, cluttered, and closed off except for a few rooms. But the sale commission is not worth Christie's effort to ferret them out, and they figure the most valuable items have already been used to settle Fallon's gaming debts."

"The family has an infamous history," Maria said, "and Percival is the worst of a bad lot. He is so ravaged by an unmentionable disease that he cannot appear in public, so he invites other heathens for weeklong bouts of gambling and . . . well, never you mind the rest. From what I understand, he is nearly gone mad from his illness, and his repellent guests have probably carried off everything of value."

"Oh." Francesca tried to absorb all these fascinating revelations. "So it's possible the book may still be there, hidden under the clutter. It is quite valuable and ought to fetch a decent sum at auction, but I would pay far more. If he knew of my interest, would the marquess conduct a search or tell us who owns it now?"

"Naturally I paid a call on your behalf," Hatchard said, "but Fallon was rather too inebriated for coherent discussion. Our best hope is that he did, in fact, use the book in payment of a debt. Unless the new owner has a particular fondness for Petrarch's sonnets, it will eventually come up for sale again."

But will Papa be alive by then? Francesca thought with a shot of pain. Will there be time for him to hold it in his hands, remembering how Mama used to read to him, in her musical Italian, the sonnets Petrarch addressed to his Laura?

One year, as a birthday surprise, Papa set out to write a love sonnet for Renalda. Every night after supper, he shut himself in the library, remaining there for hours on end. Francesca, eight at the time, had been exceedingly curious about this odd behavior. Most evenings she crept to the door and listened in, using a trick involving a drinking glass that one of the maids had taught her. But all she ever heard was a great deal of stomping about and unfamiliar words like *dammit*.

Papa never actually produced a poem.

No secret could be kept from Renalda, though. Each morning she removed the scraps of paper from his trash basket and read the ink-smudged, crossed-out lines. Francesca had discovered those papers after her mother died, bundled together under the pillow on her sickbed. Now they were her own most treasured possession. While Papa's images and rhymes were beyond

71

dreadful, his love shone through like stars on a clear, bright night.

Maria plucked at her sleeve, and Francesca wrenched her attention back to Mr. Hatchard.

". . . marquess turned me away the second time I called," he was saying, "and refused to spare another second for a mere tradesman. His language cannot be repeated, but I'll not be welcomed there again. He opens his doors only to gamesters."

"Has he family you can deal with?" she asked with a sinking heart.

"Only a son, who departed years ago for India. Or the Indies. I cannot recall which. But be assured that I have not abandoned hope, Miss Childe. If the book is no longer in Fallon's possession, there is an excellent chance I will find it."

"Thank you. It's to be a gift for my father, who is not in good health. Be assured that I shall cover any expenditure required for a speedy and thorough search." She mustered a smile. "What a splendid shop, Mr. Hatchard! Pardon me while I collect the books I have already decided to buy and select a few more, too."

With a knowing look at her face, Maria quickly drew Mr. Hatchard away, leaving Francesca to find a place to be alone in the crowded store.

How infuriating! Her precious Petrarch was in the hands of the Marquess of Fallon or one of his abominable friends, not a one of whom would recognize its value. On a cold night, the current owner might well feed it to the fire. What gamester ever cared a fig for books?

Eyes burning, Francesca reached for her handkerchief and dove into a narrow space between two shelving cases before the tears began to fall.

She nearly collided with a born gamester.

He had a book in his hands.

* * *

Clay, lurking in a dim aisle while he eavesdropped on Francesca's conversation, barely had the presence of mind to grab a book from the shelf when she suddenly turned in his direction. He flipped it open, pretending to be absorbed in the text as she came to a halt inches from where he stood.

Even in the shadow of the tall bookcases, he could see through his lashes that tears were welling in her eyes. Oh, damn.

A heartbeat later, her chin went up. "You!"

He raised his head, trying to look surprised, but the first real sight of her in a fortnight sent all his senses reeling. Unaccountably, his boots felt too tight. So did his neckcloth. And his breeches, which made more sense. Francesca Childe had been ruling his every waking thought and most of his dreams, but she was a million times more beautiful than he remembered.

Slowly, as if their meeting were taking place underwater, he watched her draw herself up to full, glorious height and level a blistering gaze at him. He waited for her to speak, so that he could summon a charming reply, but she only glared at him as if sheer scorn would make him go away.

Stampeding wildebeests could not have moved him from that spot. He bowed, awkwardly, over the book now clutched to his chest and forced polite words from a constricted throat. "How fortunate we should meet again, Miss Childe. I have wondered how you fared after the snowstorm, but obviously you made it to London in fine fettle."

"Whatever are you doing in a bookshop?" she fired back.

"Why, I wish to buy a book, of course." Mildly insulted, he raised the impressively large tome as evidence.

A light scent, like rainwater and lilac, registered on his senses as she moved closer to examine it. He traced the source to her thick black hair, which was barely contained under a rain-wilted bonnet. Such beautiful hair, he thought, imagining it spread out on a satin pillowcase.

"You read Italian?" she asked in surprise.

He glanced down at the text, seeing the words for the first time. Immediately the blood that had begun to gather below his waist shot to his head. He was fairly sure his ears had gone on fire.

"I've not yet decided if this will suit my purposes," he said evasively. "But I must confess that I was momentarily distracted, Miss Childe, when I chanced to overhear some of your conversation with John Hatchard. Mind you, I caught only a few words, relating to a book you wish to find, but you seemed distressed by what he told you."

"Which relates to the book you are holding—?"

"In no way whatsoever." He put it back on the shelf. "I do apologize for my poor manners, Miss Childe. And I confess to snatching the nearest book to hand when you came in my direction, for use as a shield. To no effect, I gather."

"None. But I still wonder why you are here at all." She frowned. "Have you been following me?"

His pulse raced. "Whyever would I do such a thing?"

"No reason," she said after giving it some thought. "I, too, apologize. The news Mr. Hatchard conveyed has overset me, and I am not thinking clearly. Of course you have every right to be in a bookshop. Please continue to browse." She made a slight curtsy. "I must find Mrs. Beaton. Good day, my lord."

Without thinking, Clay reached out for her arm. "Is there anything I can do to help?" he blurted. "Perhaps I can find what you are looking for. It happens I know

74

the Marquess of Fallon, and I have spent time at his estate."

"No doubt." She pulled away and brushed her sleeve where his hand had been. "A favored haunt for drunkards and gamblers, or so I understand. But unless you have won or carted off books from his library, you cannot assist me. Do you now own any of Fallon's books?"

"I'm afraid not. But please reconsider my offer, Miss Childe. While I no longer frequent Fallon's house parties, I have fr ... acquaintances who do. There is a good chance I can trace the book, so long as you provide a description."

She regarded him with new interest. "Perhaps you are right. Since the marquess appears unwilling to conduct business through normal channels, unusual measures may be called for. Perhaps I should recruit a libertine to handle the negotiations."

"Exactly!"

"Some *other* libertine," she specified. "You will not do, Lord Clayburn."

"But why?" If Francesca required a rakehell, what was wrong with the one standing in front of her? Finding the book she wanted would give him an excuse to see her again. And let him prove that he was, in fact, a *reformed* libertine. Well, to be strictly accurate, on his way to reformation. But surely that counted for something. "I truly wish to be of service to you," he said earnestly.

Her eyes widened. And then her lips turned up at the corners, as if she were enjoying a private joke at his expense. "Because your father has commanded it?" she inquired too sweetly.

Clay nearly swore aloud. She knew. Well, how could she not? All London had been talking about the repurchased army commission for weeks. "Whatever you have heard," he said between his teeth, "it is unlikely to be the truth. And in any case, Montford has nothing whatever to do with us."

"If you say so, Lord Clayburn. And should I ever require the services of a coxcomb, you will definitely be on my list of candidates." She examined the book he'd returned to the shelf. "Oh my. Machiavelli's *Discourses*. You might learn something, were you able to read it."

Clay watched her walk away with an imperious, purely feminine flounce. So tall and proud and confident, his goddess. His beautiful, desirable goddess. The blood in his flushed cheeks and neck began a southward journey back to his loins.

He reckoned that his blood had better get used to these round trips between humiliation and lust, since Francesca seemed to inspire both in equal measure.

She felt a strong response to him, too, he was fairly certain, although she tried to pretend it didn't exist. Something hot and bright, like heat lightning, had ignited the air around them.

It frightened her. He wanted to think so, anyway. It sure as the devil scared *him*. So much that he was willing to change his life for her.

Not a great sacrifice, certainly. And he'd set out to change before he even met her, hoping a few years in Wellington's army would give some purpose to his existence. More likely, the first battle would have put an end to it.

Despite the scandal, he was no longer sorry Montford had squelched his impulsive plan. Had he taken his place with the Fifty-second, he would never have met Francesca.

Now to discover where she lived. He peered around the bookshelf and saw her standing at the counter next to Maria Beaton, watching a clerk wrap the book she had been carrying.

While her back was turned, he swiftly exited the shop and swung left on Piccadilly, spotting a hack in front of the Egyptian Museum just a few doors away. The slumping driver perked up when Clay tossed him a coin.

"In the next few minutes," Clay directed, "two ladies will emerge from Hatchard's. One is wearing a blue pelisse. I'll let you know when I see them. Most likely they are traveling in a private carriage, but they may summon a hackney. In any case, I want you to follow them."

The jarvey spat on the pavement. "Sounds havey-cavey to me, guv. I don't want no trouble."

"Nothing of the sort. I merely wish to send flowers to a beautiful woman who was kind enough to advise me about a book." Clay passed up another coin. "Help me discover where she lives, and I'll double your fee. But be discreet. I don't want to alarm her."

"She won't ever know we is on her trail," the driver promised. "Rap on the panel when you spot 'er. I'll take it from there."

Clay swung into the cab and sat by the window, which gave him a good view of Hatchard's. Soon Maria Beaton appeared and spoke to a servant waiting on the benches in front of the shop, presumably dispatching him to have her carriage brought around. Francesca joined her on the pavement to wait.

When the coach drew up a few minutes later, Clay rapped on the panel and the chase began. But very soon the jarvey drew up curbside and leaned down to speak to him.

"They're just ahead, stopped in front of a house on Grosvenor Square. What next, guv?"

"Good man! Drive past, slowly enough so I can see the address. Then take me back to Hatchard's."

When the hackney lumbered by, Francesca was standing at the top of the stairs leading to a large town house, waving good-bye to her friend. Clay tilted his hat over his face, drinking in what little he could see of her without drawing her attention.

Then she was out of sight, until the next time. It would be soon, he promised himself, leaning back against the squabs and folding his arms. He required an excuse to call, but surely he could devise something to get him through the door. He would think on it tonight.

And begin his poem, of course. Of a sudden, images flooded into his mind, all color and light, so ephemeral he could not begin to capture them in words. Not yet.

But he knew then, of a sudden and without question, why he needed her. Why she was the woman he had never imagined wanting . . . until he met her.

He had grown up in a house of ice, and she was fire. The only woman he had ever loved, his mother, had always been weak and compliant, but Francesca was strong and confident. And although she despised him now, it was only for the same reasons he despised himself.

A painful laugh rumbled in his chest. On the subject of his flaws, if nothing else, they were in accord.

Chapter 8

Bid her come forth,
Suffer her self to be desir'd.
                    —*Edmund Waller*

"Oh, Bromley!" Francesca followed her uncle down the passageway to the entrance hall. "I wish you would not."

"No harm in it," he said, pulling on his gloves. "What's more, can't say I blame the chit for wanting to escape this madhouse. All that banging and shouting gives me the headache."

Not to mention his daily consumption of wine and brandy, she thought crossly. Bromley's arrival last night had been unexpected and disconcerting, mainly because he was looking altogether too pleased with himself. That never boded well. "Where have you been staying, Uncle?" she asked bluntly.

"Here and there, m'dear, here and there. More to the point, where in blazes is that girl?"

Just then Livvy pelted down the stairs, her flimsy muslin skirt plastered to her legs.

Francesca could scarcely believe her eyes. The goosecap had actually dampened the fabric, in the middle of winter, for an afternoon excursion with her father!

Bromley scowled. "Whatever are you thinking, widgeon? 'Tis devilish cold outside. Go put on something with a bit of substance, and be quick about it."

Grumbling loudly, Livvy slogged back up the staircase.

Arrested by this uncharacteristic show of paternal discipline, Francesca felt a spark of hope. Perhaps this excursion would not, after all, turn into the disaster she feared. "Where have you in mind to take her?" she asked.

"Oh, the Tower, I expect. After that, who can say? At some point I shall have a nip from my flask, and when 'tis emptied, I'll not be so particular where I land. Give the brat a little money, Cesca. She may be required to make her way home without me."

The spark flamed out. "Please don't let that happen, Bromley. At the very least, take Ann along as company for Livvy if your own plans change."

"Won't go," he said. "I did ask her, by the by, but I knew what she'd say. Ann's a good child, quiet and proper like her mama. I expect she'll wed a vicar or some polite stay-at-home fellow and raise a passel of brats. You find Ann a nice young gentleman, Francesca, and one for yourself, but never you mind about Livvy. She will go her own way."

Francesca, who had rarely seen Bromley sober or heard him speak sensibly, was astonished when he seized her hand and gazed steadily into her eyes.

"Livvy takes after me," he said, "to her great misfortune. She is quite as rattle-pated and even more self-willed, with no thought beyond the pleasure of the moment. You cannot change her, m'dear. You cannot even help her."

"But surely I must guard her reputation whilst we are in London. She is my responsibility."

"Ah, there you are quite wrong, Cesca. Whatever you are thinking, I assure you that Sotherton never meant you to salvage the unredeemable branch of the family. The angel Gabriel could not do that. We are merely an excuse to pry you from his sickroom long enough to find a husband."

She nodded with ill grace. Papa saw her through the distortion of a father's love, wanting for her what he'd found for himself. But the whimsical vision of a love match for his tall, ungainly daughter would never materialize. She was at her last prayers, for pity's sake.

"Do cease grinding your teeth," Bromley complained. "If it eases your mind, I've an invitation that will take me out of London the day after tomorrow. Lord Heston tells me that our host possesses an excellent wine cellar and invariably loses at cards and dice, so I expect to be gone for a considerable time." He winked. "And return considerably plumper in the pockets."

That would be a change, Francesca thought as Livvy arrived in her usual flurry, wearing her new claret-colored pelisse. The fur collar framed her pretty, stubborn face to advantage, and her blue eyes shone with the prospect of an adventure.

Since there was nothing else to be done, Francesca smiled. "You look exceptionally lovely, my dear. Wait here a moment longer, please. I have something for you."

She rushed to the library, which she had been using as an office, and unlocked the desk drawer that held a few guineas and banknotes. But by the time she arrived again in the foyer, Livvy and Bromley had departed.

Not altogether surprised, she returned to the library, where the morning post waited unopened on her desk. Bromley had interrupted her just as she was beginning to sort through an impressive stack of invitations.

Word spread fast in London, she thought. Only

two days ago, no one knew she existed. Now, after the calls she had made in Maria Beaton's company, her only problem was deciding which balls and routs to attend.

Discovering a letter from Papa buried near the bottom of the pile, she slipped it into her pocket for a later reward and broke the seal on the first invitation. Was Lady Drummond-Burrell anyone of importance? she wondered. And what would she make of Livvy Childe?

Half an hour later, Francesca threw up her hands in dismay. Except for the five women she had already met, she failed to recognize a single name among her would-be hostesses. How could she be in four places at once on Friday next, for heaven's sake? And which three of the four ladies would be most insulted by a refusal?

"Miss Childe?" The butler appeared at the door, which she had failed to close. "Three gentlemen have come to call. I put them in the Green Salon."

"I beg your pardon? We are not receiving guests, Peters."

"Perhaps they failed to notice that the knocker is not fixed upon the door. In any case, there are *three* of them and only one of me. They were most persistent."

"Remind me to acquire a large, nasty dog," she muttered, pushing away from the writing table. "Very well, I shall speak with them. Did they give you their names?"

"As to that, ma'am, I offered the tray for their cards, but they allowed as how they forgot to bring them. Then I asked their names, and they looked me up and down as if I'd been impertinent. Otherwise, they appear to be proper gentlemen."

No expert on men, proper or otherwise, she decided that the shabby brown dress she'd worn to inspect the carpenters' progress in the ballroom would do for a trio of uninvited, anonymous callers.

When Peters opened the door to the Green Salon, two young men immediately stepped forward and bowed. Although they looked vaguely familiar, she was unable to recall where she had seen them before. Then she spotted the tall, broad-shouldered figure standing near the bay window, hands clasped behind his back.

Clayburn. Her own personal Nemesis.

His father must have some dreadful hold over him, she thought disdainfully, a grip so compelling it had forced a proud man to pursue a woman who wanted no part of him.

Still, some parts of him were rather appealing. Very well, they were spectacular. When she'd ninety years on her plate and her spoon all but stuck in the wall, she would doubtless remember him as the most beautiful man she had ever seen. And perhaps wonder how it might have been to do unmentionable things with him.

Not that she would, of course. Her mother had done those things with a man who soon abandoned her to the streets, leaving Francesca with a good idea what to expect from heedless, immoral rakes.

Unfortunately, Renalda's hot blood ran in her veins. The Italian Inheritance, she'd named it years ago, a pepper-broth of temper and love of music, poetry and devotion to family, and, inevitably, the lusts of the flesh. But so far, those had only tormented her in her dreams.

She fully meant to keep it that way, in spite of Lord Clayburn's unspoken intentions. Sooner or later, she knew, he would ask her to marry him. And apparently he meant to do so in person this time, not by way of his father's letters to her father.

Clayburn was not at all what she'd imagined when Papa read her the earl's starchy communications, which were more in the way of legal briefs than letters. She had always pictured the heir as a skinny, spotty young man, the top of whose head barely reached her shoulders, a fellow who spoke with a decided lisp. The sort who could only secure a marriage of convenience, and only if the bride never saw him beforehand.

Now, confronted with this tall, splendidly muscled body, perfectly outlined by tight doeskin breeches and a well-fitted dark blue frock coat, she wondered why he let himself be manipulated in such a way by his father.

Francesca suddenly realized that she had been staring at him for God only knew how long ... with her mouth hanging open. Snapping it shut, she cleared her throat to get his attention, rather sure he had been well aware of her from the moment she entered the room.

"Miss Childe," he said, turning slowly to face her. "How kind of you to receive us."

While she had been air-dreaming, his two friends must have moved closer. She was now all but surrounded by men.

"You already know me," Clayburn continued with a wry grin. "May I present the Honorable Jeremy Porter and the Honorable Bertram Porter? Although they happen to be my friends, I assure you they are in general more discriminating."

"Gentlemen," she murmured with a curtsy, scheming how to be rid of them in the shortest possible time.

"Is Miss Ann Childe at home?" Jeremy Porter inquired politely. "We chanced to meet a few weeks ago, when taking refuge from a storm at the Rose and Thistle, and I wish to pay my regards."

Ah! So *that's* where she had seen him before. These jackals must travel in a pack.

Clayburn feigned a cough, staring meaningfully at Bertram.

"What?" Bertram asked, flushing.

"Didn't you tell me on the way here of your eagerness to see Miss Olivia Childe again?"

"Oh. Yes. Sorry." Bertram turned to Francesca. "If she is available, I am supposed to ask her for a dance."

"At Lady Sefton's ball," Clay reminded him.

"Right. I'll dance with Miss Ann Childe, too, if she likes. And you, Miss Francesca. Miss Childe. Drat it all. I can't keep the names straight." He glared at Clay. "This was your idea. *You* do the pretty."

Deliberately turning her back to Clayburn, Francesca smiled at Jeremy and Bertram. "Excuse me for a moment, gentlemen. Livvy is not home at present, but I shall go find Ann and see to refreshments."

After dispatching a servant for tea and sherry, she located Ann in the upstairs parlor, embroidering a pillowcase. Ann's face lit up when she heard that Jeremy Porter was downstairs, wishing to renew their acquaintance.

Francesca blocked her precipitous rush to the salon. "I do not fancy stirring up trouble," she said, "but the young man obviously consorts with reprobates. Exactly how did you meet him, Ann? What passed between you?"

"Must you spy an ogre around every corner, Cesca? Not all men are like my father, you know. I chanced to encounter Jerry at the inn while you were asleep, when I went in search of Livvy. He was most considerate."

Jerry? One meeting and she called him by a nickname! Oh my. Francesca decided to leave that alone for now. "Considerate he may have been. But he failed to tell you where Livvy could be found, although he knew very well that she was in the gaming room with Lord Clayburn. A man who begins by deceiving will continue to deceive, Ann. You must not trust him."

"He might have lied to me, I suppose, or simply withheld information out of loyalty to his friend. I shall keep it in mind. But truly, I would like to see him again. May I?"

For all the alarms sounding in her head, Francesca could not bring herself to disappoint Ann. "Of course you may. Go ahead of me and dish up the tea, will you? I'll be down shortly."

Propelled by a disconcerting rush of vanity, Francesca fled to her bedchamber and spent a frantic few minutes washing her face and rebraiding her hair. She longed to change her dress, but knew that would give Clayburn entirely the wrong impression.

When she reentered the Green Saloon, Bertram and Jeremy were propped like bookends on the divan with Ann seated primly between them, smiling at something one of them had said. Then she made a reply, and both young men broke out laughing.

Francesca paused, considering this wonder. Shy Ann, who had never said boo to a goose, seemed perfectly at ease with all this unaccustomed male attention.

Unwilling to disturb them, she looked around for Lord Clayburn. He was standing by the bay window, gazing out over the winter-brown garden at the back of the house. His dark hair shone in the pale sunlight, and she took an extra moment to enjoy the slight lift of his tailed coat as it curved around his taut buttocks.

She could have this man.

Stop it, Francesca! Such foolishness. Lord Clayburn might be an especially magnificent incarnation of the devil, but he was a demon nonetheless. And demons must be exorcised.

But how? He'd been clever, even coaching his friends to draw Ann into the room and keep her there. Under the circumstances, she could not precisely order him from the house.

But she might be able to freeze him out. "Shall I pour you some tea, my lord?" she inquired, hoping she sounded a hundred degrees colder than she felt.

He turned, his silver eyes gleaming with amusement. "Thank you, madam, but no. Appearances to the contrary, I do understand that you are not receiving. And that even if you were, I should not be welcome here."

"But here you are," she observed incontrovertibly. "And I daresay you hear the clatter from upstairs. Between the carpenters and the painters, the household is all at sixes and sevens."

"Point taken, Miss Childe. But since I have already intruded, allow me to present my excuses for doing so." He lifted a quizzical brow. "Or would you prefer to know the *real* reason I have come?"

"Oh, do begin with the excuses," she said, trilling a laugh that must have come from somebody else. Livvy trilled in just that fashion. Francesca steadied her voice. "As it happens, I adore fiction."

"Very well, then, we shall start at the bottom and work our way toward the light. Transparent and shabby though they certainly are, I devised reasonable pretexts for dragging my friends along with me. Oh, and I confess to intimidating your butler when he tried to turn us away. You must forgive all three of them, Miss Childe. Only *I* am responsible for cutting up your peace."

"I never doubted that for a moment, sir." She was

finding it difficult to repress a laugh. Such feigned charm and fake sincerity, from a master of both! "May I hear the reasonable pretexts?"

"To be sure." He held up a pair of fingers. "Item one has already been mentioned by Bertie, who is, by the way, more sensible than he sounds and extremely good ton. Figuring that the twins would make their first appearance at Lady Sefton's ball, I set myself to ensure they would not lack for partners. Jerry and Bertie wish to claim the first two dances, which will give the young ladies a bit of confidence when they find themselves among strangers." He lowered his index finger. "Are you impressed?"

"Mildly." In fact, she had worried herself to a nub imagining Ann and Livvy among the wallflowers all evening. "It was kind of you to make this effort on their behalf," she admitted, "although I expect you have ulterior motives."

"Oh, I do," he said without a trace of remorse. "But back to the pretexts." He waved his middle finger. "Item two. You are attempting to locate a book, and I still very much want to help you find it."

"Can you possibly have mistaken me, Lord Clayburn? I declined your assistance."

"Indeed. But should you ever require anything at all of me, send word to this address." He retrieved a slim golden case from his pocket and pulled out an engraved card. "Whatever you ask, I will do . . . with one notable exception. Which leads me to the primary reason for this unwelcome call."

She accepted his card and stared at the address he'd inscribed on the back in bold, slashing strokes. "And that would be . . . ?"

"I wanted above all things to see you again," he said simply.

Had she not known the truth of the matter, she

might well have believed that flattering declaration. His eyes, before she forced herself to look away, had held just the right touch of earnest conviction. Oh dear. Safer by far to move quickly on, she decided, sliding the card into her pocket. "And if I wish a favor, Lord Clayburn, what is the one thing you will not grant me?"

"The thing you most want, I fear. But do not ask me to keep my distance, Miss Childe, for you may be sure I'll not obey."

Oh dear, she thought again with the minuscule part of her brain that was still functioning. *Hallelujah,* the rest of her sang to Handel's music. *Hallelujah!*

Clayburn obviously recognized a good exit line when he spoke it. Rather like a border collie herding sheep, he expeditiously separated his friends from Ann and steered them out the door.

It all happened so unexpectedly that Francesca had no chance to give Clayburn the sharp setdown he deserved. The last thing she saw was Jeremy Porter casting sheep's eyes at Ann, who gazed back with disgusting adoration.

Oh, surely not Jeremy! Today he'd let himself be used as a pawn in Clayburn's game. He consorted with reprobates.

But Ann was wise enough to take the measure of his character and entitled to have some fun. Francesca reluctantly decided to let their flirtation run its course without meddling.

As for Clayburn . . . Well, what harm could it do to lead him on for a short time? It would be amusing to observe a master of seduction at work. Dangerous, to be sure, but there was no chance whatever that he would succeed. She knew full well he was acting on his father's behalf, wooing a parcel of land while pretending to court the woman who came with it.

A man like that deserved to be made to jump through hoops. Besides, he was the one who'd sworn to seek her out again, so what happened thereafter was his own fault. Why not allow Clayburn to imagine she found him irresistible? He assumed that she would. And then, when he thought the prize within his grasp, she would send him packing.

Oh, for shame, Francesca! How can you even *think* anything so mean-spirited? Gathering her skirts, she fled upstairs to distract herself by wrangling with the carpenters.

But all the while, she could not help anticipating her next encounter with Lord Rakehell. It was certain to come. And in a battle of wits, she was certain to win.

Ah, but what would she do if he carried the battle to lower ground? she wondered with a thrill of fear. What if he set upon her treasonous body, or laid siege to her lonely heart?

Dare she risk all to experience, however briefly, those hot, prickly, utterly baffling feelings he conjured with the slightest glance in her direction?

No!

Well, possibly. Even probably.

She sighed. Why lie to herself?

Yes.

Chapter 9

When the bonny blade carouses,
Pockets full, and spirits high.
                            —Samuel Johnson

Bright, early-spring sunlight streamed into the parlor where Francesca and Ann sat, listening for a knock at the door. Conversation had all but died out hours ago, and the only sound was the scratching of needles through the linen stretched on their embroidery frames.

It was a way to pass the time, Francesca supposed, wincing as the needle dug again into her forefinger. She could easier walk a high wire than embroider Papa's initials without leaving the handkerchief stained with her blood.

"You mustn't worry," Ann said for the twentieth time that day. "Young gentlemen prefer to be out and about. I expect he was not at home to receive the message."

"Indeed. It is foolish to sit here waiting for him, I know. But there is nothing else to be done."

Most likely he would see her note tomorrow morning, Francesca thought sourly, when he staggered home after a night of carousing. But she had, without reason, assumed he would materialize immediately. Wasn't there a saying to that effect? "Summon the devil and he will appear."

Apparently the devil had other plans for the day.

With a sigh, she examined the lopsided *S* she had created and began to pull out the thread for another try.

The standing clock had just chimed three when Peters entered the drawing room, a calling card on the salver in his hand and Lord Clayburn close on his heels.

Francesca stood, relief whipping through her like a March wind. "Thank you, Peters. That will be all. Please see that we are not disturbed."

Clayburn stepped forward and bowed. "Pardon my deplorable manners, Miss Childe. I should have waited to be announced, of course. And forgive me for the delay. Your message was delivered hours ago, the landlord informed me, but I only just returned home."

"Pray do not apologize, my lord. You are most kind to have come at all. Please be seated. Would you care for tea or a glass of sherry? You remember Ann Childe, I presume." Francesca bit her tongue to stop from babbling on.

Now that he was finally there, she perversely wished him elsewhere. Wished she hadn't sent for him at all. She had sworn never to do so. Contrarily, he looked very much like the answer to her prayers, strong and calm and capable of handling even this hopeless situation.

You are delusional, she told herself as he greeted Ann with a smile. Any tall man wearing a caped greatcoat looks imposing. Under all that wool, Clayburn is the same irresponsible rakehell he has always been.

But under desperate circumstances, even a rake could prove himself useful. She required only a few answers, after all, perhaps a little advice, and certainly a promise of silence. Any one of the three would be more than she expected from him.

Realizing that he was gazing at her with a puzzled expression, she gestured to a chair.

"No, thank you," he said, stripping off his gloves. "This must be something out of the ordinary, or you'd not have called for my assistance. How can I help you, Miss Childe?"

Grateful for his straightforward manner, she set herself to match it. "This morning we learned that Livvy has once again gone out in company with Lord Bromley. I hoped you might have some idea where they could be."

"I'm afraid not." He frowned. "Surely an afternoon excursion under her father's protection is harmless enough. Have you reason to be concerned?"

She retrieved a sheet of paper from her pocket. "Perhaps you should read this."

He skimmed the brief note, which was signed with a large *L*.

By now, Francesca had Livvy's words by heart. "I am off to a big estate with Father. We might be there a few days or maybe all week. Tell everyone I am sick. I don't need to appear at balls any longer. You must not go into a tizzy, Cesca. I'm perfectly safe, and Father says we will have lots of fun."

"I see," Clayburn said.

He gave her a smile that was meant to be reassuring, but she had seen his hands tighten when he read the note. He understood the implications as well as she did.

"It is inexcusable," he continued in an unruffled voice, "for Lord Bromley to take the girl away without consulting you or leaving notice of their direction. But this may be nothing more than an impulsive departure for a perfectly innocuous house party. In the weeks before Easter, many fine families prefer to entertain at their country estates."

Did Clayburn think her such a slowtop, to be mollified with absurd explanations? "And precisely which of these fine families would know of Bromley Childe?" she inquired tartly. "You have taken his measure. Is he like to be a welcome guest at a fashionable country estate?"

"Hardly." Clayburn gave her a faint smile of apology. "I suspect, as you do, that he has gone to a place no father should take his daughter. Lord knows he gave no thought to Livvy's reputation at the inn where we first met. Nor did I," he added quickly, as if expecting Francesca to leap in with a reminder.

This would all be a great deal simpler, she thought as he read the letter again, if it were possible to ignore the unspoken matters that lay between them. But she must, so long as she required his help.

"What does she mean about not needing to go to any more balls?" he asked, dropping the letter onto a side table.

"I have no idea. She's only been to one, last night at Lady Sefton's, and she never lacked for partners. But now that I think of it, she said little on the way home. That is strikingly out of character. In general, Livvy is forever rabbiting on."

"I thought it odd, too," Ann said in a quiet voice. "She had a strange, rather dreamy look on her face. I tried to talk with her about the ball while we were dressing for bed, but she seemed to be off in a world of her own."

Livvy has met a man, Francesca thought immediately. But *which* man? Only young Bertram Porter had danced twice with her, probably because Clayburn had ordered him to. And his duty done, he'd hastily taken his leave.

Francesca liked Bertram, but he was not the sort of man to put stars in the eyes of a young, excitable female. Only someone edgy and a bit dangerous, like Clayburn, would appeal to Livvy.

"I think we should focus on Bromley," Clayburn said. "Did he mention plans to leave town?"

"Yes, but mind you, he's been gadding about since we arrived in London. He reappeared a few days ago and assured me he would soon be off again. There was something about dice and an excellent wine cellar. Since reading Livvy's note, I've gone over his words again and again, but I'm sure he never said who owned that wine cellar. It is my impression he was invited secondhand, by someone whose name I cannot recall."

"It was mentioned?"

"In passing, but I never imagined it would be of importance. I'm fairly certain it started with an *H*, though, and that it had two syllables. Hickox? Halbert? Hilton?"

Clayburn, who had been pacing the room, suddenly froze. "Heston?"

"Yes! That was it. Heston. Do you know him?"

"As it happens, I do. We—"

"Livvy danced with Lord Heston last night," Ann interrupted. "I remember because he asked me first, but there was something about him that was not quite pleasing, so I told him I was on my way to the retiring room. I had to go there, of course, once I'd made the excuse. But on my way, I looked back and saw him take the floor with Livvy."

Francesca's heart sank. "This isn't good, is it?" she asked Clayburn.

"No," he said after a moment. "Whatever your opinion of me, Miss Childe, you would find Heston even more detestable. Still, he has little to gain by seducing Livvy, and he never exerts himself unless there is profit to be had. I expect he told Bromley about the gaming party, recognizing a pigeon ripe for the plucking."

"But Bromley hasn't any money."

"Not at the moment, perhaps. But he has prospects. His vowels are accepted because he stands to inherit the Sotherton title and fortune."

Francesca swallowed her response. Anyone holding Bromley's vowels would be vastly disappointed, since the Sotherton fortune was willed to her. And she'd no intention of using a groat of it to pay off any man's debts of honor. Was ever a term so ridiculous as that? What could be remotely honorable about gaming away a family inheritance or the bread from a child's mouth on the turn of a card?

Perhaps she ought to have made Bromley's exact situation known in London, if only to keep the River Tick from swallowing him up. But even thinking about her future inheritance, let alone speaking of it, was utterly repugnant. If she had her way about it, Papa would live forever.

"It's possible I may be able to learn where Heston has gone," Clayburn said reflectively. "Ought we to assume Bromley has landed in the same place, or should I mount a search for him elsewhere? That will be more difficult, I expect. He is not admitted to the clubs or known to most of my acquaintances."

"He often veers off in the most unlikely directions," she replied, "but I'm fairly certain he aimed first at the place Heston invited him."

"Very well. Give me a couple of hours, then. I understand your concern for Livvy's reputation, so be assured that the Childe name will not be mentioned in my inquiries. Have you a carriage at your disposal?"

She nodded, aware his mind had leaped several leagues ahead of hers.

"Then tell your driver to be prepared to leave on a few minutes' notice. I suggest you gather up a few things, since you may be obliged to spend the night at an inn. Doubtless you'll wish to come along."

"Oh, yes," she managed from a dry throat.

"And I!" Ann said, jumping to her feet.

"Certainly." Clayburn smiled. "I already have a fairly good idea where they can be found, but allow me to verify my hunch before we set out."

"Is it very far?" Francesca asked. "And how are we to extricate Livvy without creating a scene?"

"If the weather holds, we can be there within two hours. As for the rest, you may safely leave it to me." He bowed. "I shall return as soon as possible, Miss Childe. Try not to worry."

A few hours before midnight, Clay set out on horseback for the two-mile ride from the Black Dove Inn to Wolvercote, country seat of the Marquess of Fallon.

Lord Heston was already there, a pair of his cronies had confirmed, along with Clarence Briggs and several other die-hard gamesters. Unsurprisingly, Bromley Childe's name had not been mentioned, nor had Clay been free to bring it up. But he was confident of finding Livvy and her feckless sire within the hour.

Although there was no moon to light the road, Clay had little trouble finding his way to Wolvercote. He had spent a score of dissipated weekends there, back when the Marquess of Fallon entertained in royal fashion. Fallon had squandered much of his fortune providing vintage wines and beautiful women to the men who traveled from London to indulge his addiction for gaming.

He'd lost even more at the tables, and now his house parties attracted only hardened punters out to glean what little remained. Clay had not joined them since the parties stopped being fun, but he had a good idea what to expect.

Gaining admission to the house would be simple enough. Extricating himself, Livvy in tow, would not.

His thoughts turned to Francesca, now ensconced at the small inn a few miles back with Ann and Jerry for company. After discovering Heston's whereabouts, he had located Jerry and brought him along, not wanting to leave the women without protection.

As it happened, it wasn't the ladies who required protection. He had barely escaped with his skin intact.

When Francesca learned he meant to go alone to Wolvercote, her immediate reaction had all but set the Black Dove ablaze. Their quarrel lasted more than an hour, and he doubted she'd let him finish a sentence the entire time.

Such a firebrand, he thought, still a bit awestruck. Eventually she had calmed, fractionally, and sent him on his way, her eyes shooting darts of flame into his back.

What a lover she would be, all that rage transformed into passion. When at last he took her into his arms and his bed, he would be the luckiest man in the universe.

But first he must pluck the recalcitrant Livvy from Fallon's private gaming hell, and possibly even from Heston's bed. He profoundly hoped things had not yet progressed to that point. When he met Heston, which was inevitable, he bloody well did not want to be fighting a duel over the likes of Livvy Childe.

Clay reined to a halt on a knoll overlooking the rambling patchwork mansion, assembled by five centuries of Fallon marquesses with wildly differing notions of architecture. Nearly the whole house was shrouded in darkness, but light streamed from the windows of the large saloon where Fallon usually set up his tables. By now, the gaming would be in full swing.

After considering several plans, he decided on the simplest approach—walk directly in, determine

Livvy's whereabouts, and improvise some way to make off with her.

Before leaving London, he had gone to his rooms long enough to change clothes and pocket the last of his funds. Four hundred pounds would buy him into the game, but the stake would last only a short time unless he got very lucky. Fallon played deep and expected his guests to do likewise.

Within a few minutes, Clay had stabled his mount and gained access to the house. A bored servant admitted him without question and escorted him down the long, meandering passageway to the gaming parlor.

"You'll be needing a bedchamber, milord," he advised by rote. "When you are ready, ask whoever is on duty to show you to the Peacock Suite. I'll see a fire is made up for you."

Clay passed him a coin and stepped through the door, blinking against the cloud of cigar smoke that all but obscured a large round table in the center of the room. He counted eight men, recognizing most of them. Sure enough, Bromley was there, seated close to Heston. Between them, a disgruntled look on her face, Livvy fidgeted on her chair.

So far so good. He sauntered to the table, bowing when a few of the gamblers glanced up from their cards to acknowledge his arrival.

Heston was the first to speak, grinning sourly. "Too hot for you in London, Clayburn?"

"Just so," he replied in an amiable voice. "For my sins, I am compelled to slum with the likes of you." Clay turned to Fallon, immediately repelled by his drink-glazed amber eyes and the narrow face pocked with open sores. "Good evening," he said with another polite bow. "May I join you?"

Fallon waved a skinny hand toward an empty chair.

"Sit down, sit down. Your money is always good here. Got any?"

"Never enough, I'm afraid."

While the men played out the current deal, he leaned back in his chair to study the situation. Bromley was already having trouble focusing on his cards. Another hour of drinking and he wouldn't notice if a horde of Mongols swept into the room and made off with his daughter. No problems from that source.

Heston was another matter. No telling if he meant to bed Livvy tonight, but from sheer perversity he would object if Clayburn showed a speck of interest in the chit.

Without question, he would have to finesse her away before anyone guessed what he was about. He drew half his small bankroll from his pocket. Everyone assumed he'd come to gamble, so for the next few hours his main concern would be to stay in the game.

Livvy waved her fan in his direction. "Hullo, Lord Clayburn. We keep meeting in the oddest places. This time I'm learning how to play macao, but they—"

A chorus of shushes interrupted her. Pouting, she leaned forward and set a possessive hand on Heston's shoulder. He batted it away as he would an insect, and she lapsed back on her chair with an audible sigh.

Clay ignored her, still evaluating his options. Too bad that Fallon had chosen macao for the evening's entertainment. A game of luck, it offered almost no chance for him to apply skill against the random fall of the cards. Not that he meant to win heavily, of course. Indeed, his half-formed plan required him to lose . . . eventually. No winner could leave the table without rousing immediate protest, and attention was the last thing he wanted.

But he required an edge, to manipulate the action, and macao didn't suit his purposes. He managed to hang even the first hour, contriving to look almost as bored as Livvy. Fortunately, the marquess had been losing steadily.

"I say, Fallon," Clay drawled when it came his turn to hold the bank. "How about if we liven things up by changing the game? Vingt-et-un, perhaps?"

Fallon jumped at the chance to reverse his run of bad luck. "Vingt-et-un it is. Agreed, gentlemen?"

Everyone knew better than to object, so Clay dealt the first hand of a game wherein he could seize an advantage by counting the cards already played and wagering accordingly. Most of the others were too drunk by now to do the same.

Another hour passed with money changing hands at rapid speed. Then Livvy spoke up in a whiny voice. "Why won't you let *me* play? This is an easy game. I've already figured it out. And I'm *bored*."

"Quiet!" Fallon glared at her. "Or take yourself off. This is no place for a squirrel-brained female."

Clay hoped she would give up and retire to her bed-chamber, where he could easily find her later. But she stayed in place, squirming and fiddling with her fan.

Play grew more intense. And when the heavy drinkers began to slide out of control, upping the stakes and betting at random, Clay was hard put to keep from losing everything. At one point, only ten guineas remained on the table in front of him.

Heston gave him a malicious smile. "About plucked dry, old sod? Pity you couldn't stay with us longer, but your vowels are no good here. Everyone knows Montford has cut you off."

Clay reached into his pocket and pulled out a sheaf of banknotes. Over his objections, Francesca had pressed the money into his hand just before he left the Black Dove. He'd never meant to use it.

Still, instinct told him it was too soon to leave the

room. And when he did, the men had to figure he was planning to return. "There is more where this came from," he said, slurring his voice. "I need a drink. Where's the bottle? Somebody deal."

He refilled his glass with an unsteady hand and contrived to pour most of the brandy on the floor while the players were busy studying their cards. The brandy joined a pool of liquid under his boots, where all but one or two earlier drinks had been deposited. This one night, he had to appear drunk and remain starkly sober.

Even Heston began to play carelessly after a while. Clay managed to win a considerable amount from him and Briggs while losing to Fallon and the others. Now and again he slipped notes back into his pocket, because he would need them later. Soon he'd recovered all of Francesca's money, along with half his own stake. That amount he kept on the table, visible to everyone.

Always, he watched Livvy closely. The chit had an overabundance of stamina, he thought with admiration. Although she drank almost as steadily as the men, it didn't seem to faze her in the slightest.

But at long last she began to raise the fan to conceal her yawns. Clay played two more hands, winning heavily on the first and losing a bit on the second. By now, a decent number of guineas were stacked on the table in front of him.

It was time.

He lurched to his feet. "Gentl'men, deal me out a li'l while. Gotta do what a man's gotta do. Call of nature, what? Better clear m'head, too. Can't tell a ten from a deuce." He swayed and put both hands on the table as if trying to regain his balance.

Livvy was sitting directly across from him, and he stared at her for a long time. Then he jabbed a finger in her direction. "Izzat a female? What's she doin' here? Thought you had better sense, Fallon. Ought to be somewhere else, I say. But if you want her here, well, so be it."

"I don't," Fallon said with a snarl. "She's been a damned nuisance all night. Take her with you, Clayburn. Have a servant put her in a room and turn the key. Make sure she don't come back."

"If you say so, m'lord." Clay pushed himself upright and staggered around in a complete circle. "Where's the bloody door? C'mon, female. Show me the way out."

For a tense moment, Clay thought Livvy would toss a fit. Then she leaned toward Heston and whispered something in his ear.

"Not now," he grumbled. "I'm playing cards."

She gave him a scorching look, bolted from her chair, and stomped to the door. "This way, Lord Clayburn. I'd rather come with you than stay here with these boors."

To his relief, Heston failed to react to her challenge. Clay waved at the guineas he was leaving behind on the table. "You wait here," he told them. " 'Bye for now. I'll see you later."

He lurched toward the door and let Livvy escort him down the passageway until they arrived in the foyer. Luckily, there was no servant in sight. "Wanna see m'horse," he said. "Nobody with any sense works for Fallon, and I don't trust that ostler."

"But it's cold outside." To his astonishment, she rubbed up against him, making sure he noticed the swell of her breasts under her thin, low-cut gown. "I'm sure the horse is fine. Perhaps we should go to bed now."

"H-horse," he insisted. This time his stammer was genuine. Did the girl mean to seduce him? Hell, if she was that eager to put her back to a mattress, he might as well leave her here with Heston.

But Olivia's virtue was none of his concern, he reminded himself. He was doing this for Francesca. Stripping off his coat, he placed it over the girl's bare shoulders and led her outside.

"Oh!" she said when they arrived at the stable. "Can that huge black be your horse? He hasn't even been unsaddled."

"How convenient." All business now, Clay slipped the ostler a half crown. "There will be another on my return. Meanwhile, you have seen nothing."

The old man bit the coin with his few remaining teeth. "Feels solid, m'lord. Can't see it 'cuz I 'appen to be blind."

Laughing, Clay swung onto the saddle and held out his arms. "Up you come, young lady."

She took a step back. "Where are we going?"

"For a ride under the stars." He gestured to the ostler, who moved behind Livvy in case she tried to bolt. "Just the two of us. I've been planning this since first I saw you in Fallon's gaming room. Perhaps before that," he added in strictest honesty. "Where would you rather be? In that smoky room where nobody pays attention to you, or up here with my arms wrapped around your waist?"

Within seconds, Livvy was settled in front of him, giggling like a schoolgirl. "I knew you liked me," she said as he guided the horse onto the road. "And you are much more handsome than Rupert, although he is very attractive, too. He said we would have a good time together if I convinced Father to bring me to Wolvercote. So I did. Supper was fun. Everybody laughed and told amusing stories. But when they all started playing cards, I might as well have been invisible."

In spite of the dark road, Clay urged his mount to a trot, in a hurry to rid himself of this chatterbox, and damnably cold in shirtsleeves and waistcoat. As further proof he meant to return, he'd thought it best to leave his greatcoat, hat, and gloves at Wolvercote.

"They kept telling me to be quiet," she continued relentlessly. "Even Rupert was beastly. He was much nicer when we danced at Lady Sefton's ball. I'm glad you came, actually. I'd much rather be with you. Even though you didn't ask me to dance at the ball last night. Why?"

"Because I didn't want to," he said between his teeth. "Shut up, Livvy. I need to concentrate on the road."

"Of course," she said.

"Where are we going?" she asked a few moments later. "This is vastly romantic, to be sure. But if we wind up back at Wolvercote, Rupert might take offense that we were alone together. He will probably call you out."

From her wriggling against his thighs, Clay reckoned she found the notion of men dueling for her favors an appealing one. "Heston and I are almost certain to face off with pistols some foggy morning," he said dryly. "But it won't be over you. Our quarrel dates back to school days, and if ever there was a reason for it, I cannot recall what it was."

"You might ask him," she suggested "He is perfectly reasonable, unless he has cards in his hands. Then he is a positive sourpuss."

Clay was more than pleased to see light directly ahead. The Black Dove. He reined the horse to a walk as they came near the entrance.

"Oh!" Livvy leaned back against his chest. "An inn. You *do* mean to be alone with me. I am so glad.

Not that I expected anything else, since you are the very model of a rake."

He dismounted and barely managed to catch her when she jumped into his arms, rubbing against his body like a harlot. Fueled by all the wine she'd drunk, she had clearly abandoned what few inhibitions she ever possessed.

Setting her at arm's length, he tapped her on the nose with an excruciatingly cold finger. "Yes, but I am a most *discriminating* rake. Now, come along. I have a surprise for you."

Chapter 10

If of herself she will not love,
Nothing can make her.
—*Sir John Suckling*

In a private parlor at the Black Dove Inn, Francesca was diligently wearing a circular track on the floorboards with her pacing.

Clayburn had been gone for hours. Aeons. She'd long since despaired of him, and only Jerry's calm objections prevented her from setting out for Wolvercote on her own.

She glanced at Jerry as she passed by the sofa where he'd sat quietly with Ann all evening, except when he left to secure fresh tea and more logs for the fire. How incongruous that such a nice young man should be Clayburn's friend.

It was past one in the morning when the door swung open with a bang.

Livvy, a man's coat draped over her shoulders, staggered into the room as if she'd been pushed. When she spotted Francesca, she emitted a loud squawk and whirled to face Lord Clayburn, who had come in behind her.

"The prodigal returneth," he said to Francesca. "Under some duress, I fear, and with a few preconceptions about my intentions in her regard. Those have just been demolished."

"Indeed they have, you brutal, lying fiend! Father will call you out for this. See if he doesn't!"

"I am quaking in my boots. Meantime, unless you relish the taste of my neckcloth stuffed in your mouth, I suggest you close it."

Francesca knew she ought to relieve Clayburn of his unwelcome charge, but the pleasure of watching Livvy being managed by an expert was too delicious.

He beckoned then to Ann and Jerry, who had risen from the sofa to observe the spectacle. "If you please, Ann, take this tiresome nitwit elsewhere and clean her up. I hope you've brought a spare gown or two, but if not, wrap her in a blanket. We were forced to leave her luggage behind, and she is wearing precious little at the moment." He whisked his coat from her shoulders. "I'll take this back now."

Francesca gasped. Livvy had been wearing *that* dress, what there was of it, in company with England's most notorious degenerates?

Livvy stomped her foot. "I demand to go back to Wolvercote! Now!"

From directly behind her, Clayburn clamped his hand over her mouth. "How unfortunate, since you will be on your way to London within the hour. Jerry, should she give you any trouble upstairs, do whatever you must to restrain her."

Ann approached her sister and brushed a windblown lock of hair from her forehead. "Come, Livvy. You are vastly outnumbered, you know. And I imagine you are excessively tired after such an eventful day. If Francesca promises not to ring a peal over you in the carriage, will you come along peaceably?"

In spite of Clayburn's tight grip over the bottom half of her face, Livvy managed a resentful nod.

Ann smiled over her shoulder at Francesca. "You do promise?"

"Oh, very well. We are all out of temper. I shall contain mine, if Livvy does the same."

"She will," Ann said confidently. "You may release her now, my lord."

Clayburn stepped away. "Miss Childe will let you know when it is time to leave, Ann. Meanwhile, we wish to be private."

With an insolent toss of her head, Livvy swept out of the room like a ship of the line under full canvas.

"Oh my," Francesca murmured as Jerry closed the door.

"She is fearless," Clayburn said. "I'll grant her that much. But Ann appears to have got all the brains in the family."

"All the heart, too." Even though the crisis seemed to be over, at least for now, her own heart was thumping at triple speed.

She had rarely been alone with a gentleman other than her father, and never with one who managed to look both elegant and disheveled at the same time. It must be damp outside, because the sleeves of his white shirt were molded to his shoulders and arms, outlining contours that suddenly fascinated her.

Under his buff-colored waistcoat, doeskin breeches clung explicitly to narrow flanks, powerful thighs, and other amazing sectors of male anatomy. For an indolent wastrel, he possessed a splendid array of muscles. With an act of will, she lifted her gaze to his face. And immediately wondered how it would feel to comb her fingers through that tousled dark hair.

Casting about for her scattered wits, Francesca realized that Lord Clayburn was staring at her with equal intensity. His coat, which had been dangling from one hand, now lay crumpled on the floor.

She thought to go pick it up but dared not go so close to him. *Say something,* she told herself, *preferably something comprehensible.* "What happened?" she asked.

He looked as though the sound of her voice had snapped him from a trance. "Ah, yes. Livvy. I had almost forgot." He strode to the fireplace and held his hands to the flames. "Forgive me for turning my back to you, madam, but it is devilish cold outside. I seem to have grown icicles where my fingers used to be."

Her tongue, which had been stuck in her throat like a log, suddenly broke loose with a vengeance. "Oh dear. I am so very sorry. And to think you permitted that vexatious girl to wear your coat. Please do thaw yourself. Shall I send for tea? Or do you prefer brandy?"

He chuckled. "I *always* prefer brandy. But nothing for now, thank you. I know you are anxious to learn what transpired at Wolvercote. It's not all good, of course. But so far as I can detect, Livvy came to no serious harm. She was in the gaming room when I arrived, watching the play and sulking because Fallon had ordered her to cease her prattling." He glanced over his shoulder. "I fear the chit has a prodigious capacity for wine. In fact, she could probably drink me under the table."

"Yet another dismal inheritance from Bromley," Francesca said with a sigh. "Did he object when you took her away?"

"*Nobody* objected. Indeed, they were all too pleased to see the back of her. Mind you, they assumed she was merely headed for her bedchamber."

"With you?"

"Hardly. Good Lord, Francesca, I hope they credit me with better taste than that!"

"Even Lord Heston?"

"Who knows what he thinks? But Livvy has him in her sights, that is certain. And anything she offers him, other than a leg-shackle, he will almost surely accept."

"Do you suppose they have already . . . ?"

His wide shoulders rose and fell as he took a deep breath. "As to that, you must ask Livvy. But I would presume not. They arrived at Wolvercote quite late in the afternoon, and she hasn't the look of a woman recently bedded."

Francesca wondered exactly how a recently bedded woman was supposed to look.

"Heston's intentions remain unclear," he said, all but straddling the fire in his effort to get warm again. "I chose not to put them to the test by making off with her in an obvious way. Not any one of those men would credit that I meant only to restore a silly girl to the bosom of her family, so a more devious strategy was in order."

"And clearly it succeeded," she said, impressed. "Will you explain it to me?"

"I'll not even try." He turned his back to the hearth and folded his arms, smiling at her. "I have some experience with sodden gamblers, having been one in my time, and that is all I mean to say on the subject."

"Was there a fight?" she couldn't help asking. "Was anyone hurt?"

Laughing, he shook his head. "Leave it alone, my dear. If there is to be trouble, which I seriously doubt, it will take place when I return to Wolvercote."

"But why would you do such a thing? Especially if there might be trouble."

"Well, to begin with, Childe must be told what has become of his daughter. At the moment he has no idea she is gone, but he's bound to notice in a day or two. Also, I lost rather a good deal of money and mean to recover it. Which reminds me . . ."

He crossed to pick up his coat and drew something

from the pocket. "A portion of this is yours. A hundred pounds, as I recall."

"Keep it!" she insisted as he began to peel off banknotes. "Heaven knows you have earned that pittance, and a great deal more besides."

His head shot up. "Do you imagine I did this for *money*?"

"N-no. But you would not have been in that game if not for me. And by your own account, you . . . Well, the very least I can do is cover your losses."

"Confound you, Francesca!"

He advanced on her, backing her up until her shoulders hit the wall. She gazed helplessly at his cravat as he planted his hands against the wall just behind her head, imprisoning her with his large body.

"There is much I want from you," he said stonily. "Far more than you can imagine. But money is no part of it. And you will never, *ever*, be in debt to me."

She could not mistake the anger radiating from him. And she knew the exact moment when he realized what he was doing. Seconds later, he stepped away, both hands lifted in a gesture of apology.

"There is no need," she told him when he began to speak. "I already understand. As it happens, I have somewhat of a temper myself."

"I had noticed." He lowered his arms. "But as a rule, I do *not* have a temper. Not one I've been unable to control, at any rate, until the last few moments."

It disturbed him, she realized, that loss of self-control. And at the same time, she was reassured to find him capable of a temper that matched her own. When they had quarreled about his solo venture to Wolvercote, she had raged at him to no purpose whatsoever. It had been like pounding her head against a glacier.

"Do you mean to rake me over the coals?" he asked

lightly. "If so, please get on about it. Waiting for punishment, I have learned, is far more painful than the actual whipping."

"Which is why I keep you waiting, of course. But in truth, I much prefer to deal with people who speak their minds, which you have done. Now I shall speak mine. Whatever you choose to believe, Lord Clayburn, I am indebted to you. Not because you demand repayment or expect it, but because I feel an obligation to return the favor you have generously performed."

"Then you feel what does not exist. There is no obligation."

"Yes, you have said so, and my mind accepts it. But I *feel*, quite inexorably, an obligation you must allow me to satisfy. Perhaps only another woman could understand."

"But then, a woman would not be distracted by wondering at the precise nature of your inexorable feelings." He moved closer, until the fabric of his waistcoat brushed against her suddenly sensitive breasts. "Let it not be said I have ever refused a lady, madam. If you demand satisfaction, then naturally I must oblige you."

It was impossible to order her thoughts with him standing so close, gazing at her in just that way. "How?" she asked feebly.

"Not with money," he said, his voice husky and suggestive. "It's quite simple what I want from you."

There was an endless, breathless pause.

And then he grinned. "The next time I ask you to dance with me, Miss Childe, you must say yes."

"B-but I cannot," she sputtered. "Dance, I mean. I told you so last night at the ball."

"Would you have danced with me if you knew the steps?"

"Probably not," she had to admit. She might have

wanted to. No, she *had* wanted to. But matronly chaperones of one-and-thirty did not take the floor with handsome young bucks. Everyone would have remarked upon it.

"May I ask why?" he inquired gently. "Or do I already know?"

No longer sure what *she* knew, Francesca could not begin to guess what went through his intricate mind. "I have never danced. I cannot perform the steps. All else is moot, Lord Clayburn, so name another favor I can perform."

He wagged his elegant eyebrows. "Now, let me see—"

"Never mind!" she interrupted hastily. "Perhaps in the future something will arise. Then you can tell me about it."

"Oh, something has risen long since," he said with a wicked glint in his eyes. "But I fear that will have to wait. Meantime, may I suggest a gamble on the futures market?"

Francesca had no idea what he was talking about. Flailing, she said the only thing that made its way intact from her brain to her tongue. "I have no idea what you are talking about."

"Speculation," he informed her. "This night's mission is done with, and that you called on me when you needed help was more than sufficient reward. Joined with the pleasure of your company, there remains some question about which of us is in debt to the other."

Apparently this was how rakes went about getting their way, she thought with annoyance. They threw handfuls of words, so fast any normal person's mind would lose track of the subject. And they stood close and looked so virile that any woman with a breath in her body wanted only to be kissed.

But wanting was not the same as doing. She squared her shoulders. "I hope you will one day come to the point, my lord."

He laughed. "Very well, if you'll stop my-lording me. Should it happen I have the good fortune to perform for you another service, one that makes you feel *inexorably obligated*, you will allow me to teach you to dance."

"Dance? Good heavens. Whatever for? I shall soon return to the provinces, where such a skill is singularly useless. And with my great height, few men would choose to partner me in any case."

"I am glad to hear it. Now have done with arguments, or I'll be forced to remind you who it was who began this absurd negotiation. The circumstance may never come to pass, you know. And if it should, I'll not take undue advantage." He gave her a coaxing smile. "Say *yes*."

"I'll say *perhaps*," she conceded reluctantly. "At the moment, I mistrust the both of us."

"Excellent. Not a great accomplishment on my part, but progress of a sort." He fingered a tendril of hair that had escaped her braid. "Last night, when I came into the ballroom, I looked everywhere for you. It was nearly an hour before I found you hiding in an obscure corner with the chaperones."

He leaned forward until his mouth was no more than an inch from hers. She thought he meant to kiss her then and shivered with anticipation.

But he only brushed her cheek with his lips. "When I saw you, shining like a torch in your red-gold gown, my heart stopped. And I wasn't at all certain it ever meant to start again."

"It must have d-done," she mumbled, unaccountably disappointed when he moved to a safer distance.

"No doubt you think I'm giving you Spanish coin,"

he said after a moment. "Even when I say words to you I truly mean, they sound false to my own ears because I've said them before, to other women, when I didn't mean them."

"I daresay."

"Well, I see you have already judged and sentenced me. And when I am gone, you'll soon convince yourself there was some self-serving motive behind everything I said and did tonight."

"There was not? People generally act in their own self-interest, I believe."

"Ah." He retrieved his coat and shoved his arms into the sleeves. "What a cynical creature you are, Francesca Childe. I wonder why. Hardened, worldly rakes like me are *supposed* to be cynical, but here I am, brimming with hope and high expectations."

And on your way to another night of debauchery, she thought irritably. "Then I must certainly take lessons in character and spiritual growth from you, Lord Clayburn."

"Shrew," he said, grinning. "I'd like to begin your education this very moment, but it's late and I must be off. Jerry will see you home safely."

A minute later, Francesca came to her senses. She rushed into the passageway and finally caught up with him in the taproom, negotiating with a farmer for a shabby pair of work gloves. Both men looked up at her in surprise.

Cheeks flaming with embarrassment, she curtsied. "Forgive me, my lord. It's just that . . . I mean . . . I never thanked you."

The farmer winked and prodded Clayburn in the ribs with his elbow. "Good goin' there, laddie. Always leave 'em happy and wantin' more, I sez."

"You sez right," Clayburn replied, handing him several coins and accepting the gloves. "There's extra

116

there for a round of drinks." Still in no great hurry, he moved to Francesca and led her into the passageway.

"What was he talking about?" she asked with a frown.

"Oh, you'll figure it out on the way back to London." He smiled warmly. "Come to thank me, did you? There is no need, but I confess to enjoying the experience."

"Yes, well, it seems I also require a lesson in manners. I am truly grateful, you know. But—" Catching herself, she fumbled for a turn of subject. "Nice gloves."

He used them to lift her chin, gazing steadily into her eyes. "But what, Francesca?"

She owed him the truth, she supposed. Or part of it. "I'm sure it is not deliberate, sir, but you bring out all the most detestable aspects of my nature. I scarcely see you but that I feel my temper hotting up. And then, of course, I am insufferably rude to you."

"So you are." He didn't seem the least bit disturbed by her revelations. "But I don't mind. It's when you go cold and insufferably polite on me that I'll begin to worry. As for now, why don't you thank me in proper fashion?"

"And how is that?" she asked suspiciously.

Immediately he swept her into his arms. "Like this," ho whispered into her ear. "Nothing more. Only a touch of your fire, to warm mo on the ride back to Wolvercote. Something to dream about, until I see you again."

Francesca felt that embrace long after he was gone. All the way to London, she felt it. And she dreamed about him, too.

Chapter 11

The lunatic, the lover, and the poet.
—*Shakespeare*

Well after noon the next day, a slovenly house-keeper led Clay along a dim passageway lined with bare peeling walls, stopping before a pair of massive oak doors, "This be it, milord. Nobody uses this part of the 'ouse anymore, and I 'spect the chimneys is clogged. Ye'll have to make do without a fire."

"Thank you for escorting me," he said, passing her a coin. Fallon rarely paid his staff, and Clay knew he must offer vails if he expected any service. "This place is a veritable rabbit warren."

"Aye. But only rats come 'ere these days." After a look that cast him firmly in the role of demented rodent, she shambled back toward the moderately habitable portion of Wolvercote.

As he pushed open the heavy doors, Clay heard the unmistakable rustle of small animals scurrying for cover. The dark, cavernous library smelled of mold and animal droppings.

Oh yes, this will be jolly good fun, he thought, crossing to the curtains at the far end of the room. The drawcord had been eaten away by something desperate for a meal, so he grabbed a fistful of heavy velvet and attempted to open the curtains by hand.

Immediately a voluminous swath of decayed fabric broke loose and enveloped him, stinking like a shroud

118

unearthed from a mummy's tomb. He threw it off, choking as clouds of dust billowed around him.

When he finally controlled his fit of sneezing, Clay realized that eliminating the curtains made precious little difference. The grimy windows allowed only the barest trace of sunlight to filter through.

At least he could see the bookcases now. They lined both sides of the library from floor to ceiling, with a pair of worm-ridden ladders set nearby to provide access to the higher shelves.

There looked to be several thousand books there, all coated with a heavy layer of dust. Clay whooshed a breath and chose the left side of the library to begin his search. He wasn't exactly looking forward to the job, but he'd already been put to a great deal of trouble for this opportunity and meant to waste not a moment of it.

By the time he reentered Fallon's gaming room last night—well, this morning, not to put too fine a point on it—only five players remained at the table. Heston and Briggs had gone off to bed, and Bromley Childe, his head resting on his folded arms, snored away while play continued around him.

Clay had immediately set out to put Fallon in his debt, which became child's play when the company dwindled further and he was able to turn the game to whist. Finally, well past dawn, after the others headed for their rooms and Bromley slid bonelessly to the floor, Clay and Fallon discussed payment.

"Books?" The marquess regarded him as if he'd grown a second nose. "You'll accept books instead of cash? Well, by all means, take any damned book you want. Take the whole bloody lot of 'em. But when you leave here, we stand even."

"Agreed. I require only permission to examine every book you own before making my final selection."

"Yes, yes. Agathy will show you around. She's the housekeeper. Look wherever you like, except my personal rooms. No books in there." Fallon barked a laugh. "I only read the Devil's Books. Playing cards. Amusing, what?"

Clay had dutifully chuckled and gone to catch a quick nap atop the counterpane in his musty bed-chamber. He woke up scratching and knew he must have provided breakfast for a host of starving insects.

At least he now had free run of Wolvercote, for as long as required to locate Francesca's book. Of course, it might not be there at all, in which case he could assure her that someone else now owned it. From what John Hatchard said, that meant it would likely come up for auction soon.

But Clay did not want another owner in the picture. He profoundly wanted to find that book himself and be the one who put it into her hands. He wanted to see her smile when she recognized what she held.

Would *he* recognize it? he wondered. He could not be sure of anything except that the book contained sonnets by Petrarch, and those were easily come by. There were even some in the anthologies he'd bought for himself at Hatchard's. The book Francesca wanted must be unique in some way, but precisely how? Perhaps it had once belonged to a famous personage who inscribed his name inside.

Well, no point worrying about it. He'd carry off every volume of Petrarch's poems he found and let Francesca sort through them herself.

By late afternoon, three dusty volumes that even he knew to be valueless lay on the table where he devoured the stale sandwiches Agathy had brought him on a tray. Absorbed by the search, he ate quickly and was soon hard at work again.

An hour or so later, he was balanced precariously on a chair, his back to the door, when he heard an unwelcome voice.

"Hullo," Rupert Heston remarked cheerfully. "Dare I ask why you are rummaging about in this catacomb?"

"Just catching up on my reading," Clay replied, the chair teetering ominously as he made a half turn in Heston's direction. "What of it?"

"Why, nothing at all. You were ever attics to let." Pressing his handkerchief to his nose, Heston gingerly stepped into the filthy room. "However do you bear this stench?"

"I detected none, until you arrived. Here's an idea. Take the odor, and yourself, away."

"In a bad mood, are we?" Heston tilted his head. "I know that I am, since you appear to have made off with Olivia Childe. Where, may I inquire, did you deposit her?"

"With her family. The reputable branch, which has some care for her reputation."

"Unlike her great looby of a father." Heston sneezed into his handkerchief. "Even I was astonished that he brought her to Wolvercote. Not altogether displeased, you understand. She is remarkably engaging when her mouth is closed, and a man in possession of a firm gag might consider pursuing the acquaintance. Not to mention that one day soon, she will be a duke's daughter. Rather boggles the mind, does it not? Bromley Childe a duke of the realm. Whatever is England coming to?"

"More relevant, is there some point to your nattering?" Clay asked impatiently.

"Probably not. I had thought, briefly, that we two were fixed on the same target. But as you are flopping about on a chair instead of romping in bed with said target, I was clearly mistaken. Or do you mean to go for the quiet twin instead? How droll. Think on it, Clayburn. Should you marry Ann and I Livvy, we would become brothers-in-law!"

"Don't count on it." Clay jumped to the floor. "Olivia has already returned to London, and you'll not find it so easy to approach her again."

"Oh, but she will come for me," Heston said confidently. "If you doubt that, you fail to understand women. The only question is, will I take her? I have not decided."

"Well, when you make up your mind, don't bother to tell me. I am profoundly uninterested in the both of you."

"How devastating. But you might be interested in my other snippet of news. Lord Philby has just arrived to join Fallon's games, bringing with him the latest *on dits* from the city. Steel yourself, old sod. Montford is in London. And he is looking for you."

Clay absorbed that blow with an indifferent shrug, although his stomach began to churn. The earl had not set foot in London for years. Why now, if not to drag his son home and shackle him to the Albatross?

"No doubt you'll wish to set out immediately," Heston said caustically. "Mustn't keep papakins waiting."

Oh, but he must, for the rest of his life if he had his way about it. He would certainly remain at Wolvercote until he'd found Francesca's book, Montford be damned.

"I understand you'd like to eliminate me from the gaming," he said, moving the chair a few feet along the bookshelves and climbing atop it again. "But I'll most certainly be there tonight, and for so long as I enjoy myself. Not easy to do in this rathole, I confess, but I'm having a good time pocketing your money."

"Ah, yes. Well, you have profited from my recent turn of bad luck, nothing more than that. And who can blame you for hiding out at Fallon's sponging house while your formidable sire waits in London to pounce?" With a mocking bow, Heston turned for the door. "Until later, then? We shall contrive to keep you entertained, if only to prevent your knees from knocking together under the table. Most distracting."

"Go to the devil," Clay said pleasantly.

Two days later, winning heavily from Heston had lost its appeal, as had the fruitless search for Francesca's book. After tedious nights at Fallon's table, Clay snatched a few hours of sleep and resumed his relentless appraisal of every book in the Library from Hell. He had even ventured to the high shelves atop those rickety ladders.

But for all his efforts, only seven books containing poems by Petrarch, not a one of them unique or valuable, had been located. By now, he smelled as putrid as the library itself, since he'd been living in the shirt, breeches, and coat he rode in wearing.

On his third afternoon in the library, as Agathy departed after plunking a tray of sandwiches on the table, she paused at the door and scratched her chin. "I dunno what you're lookin' fer," she said, "but some other gentlemen been through this room, mebbe six months ago. They took out some books and put 'em inter boxes. Said they was goin' to be suld off to auction at Christmas. Never was, though. Them boxes got put in another room with some paintings and the like. Happen you want to see 'em?"

Happen he did!

Mentally translating "Christmas" to "Christie's," Clay followed the housekeeper to an upper floor and a small room crammed with antique furniture, statuary, ornate silver epergnes, and suits of armor. Canvases were stacked against the walls, and every spare inch of floor held wooden boxes piled one on top of another, reaching almost to the low ceiling.

The room was even colder than the library, but Clay understood that a fire was out of the question. He gave Agathy another coin and asked her to fetch his greatcoat and gloves.

He had managed to clear the top of a marquetry table and a foot or so of space beside it when she returned, in company with a wiry boy about ten years of age. The urchin immediately scrambled over the barricade of furniture and boxes to open the curtains, and then perched atop a large sideboard, propping his bony elbows on his knees.

"I reckoned you could use some 'elp gettin' to the back spots," Agathy said, "you bein' a man of size." She passed Clay his greatcoat and accepted a half crown in return. "Send 'im off iffen he plagues you."

"I works cheap," the boy piped eagerly after watching the coin change hands.

"Behave yerself," Agathy warned, trundling out the door.

"Have you a name?" Clay inquired as he opened the closest box and set it on the table.

"Don't ever'body got 'un?" he replied pertly. "Mine's Jedediah," he added when Clay shot him a look of reproval. "I generally answers to Jed."

"And I generally answers to my lord or your lordship," Clay said, disappointed when the first box turned up full of saltcellars and other knickknacks. He returned it to the floor and reached for another box. "But since we are to be informal, you may call me sir."

As the day wore on, he came to be glad of the boy's

company. It was Jed who thought of moving the paintings into the passageway, clearing more space for them to work, and Jed who made frequent trips to the kitchen for mugs of hot, strong tea.

Jed also chattered incessantly, when he wasn't gulping down the biscuits Agathy sent with the tea, and Clay learned rather more than he needed to know about the life of a kitchen scouring boy. But he was interested to learn that belowstairs rivalries and *affaires de coeur* bore a striking similarity to the scandalous doings of the Haut Ton.

Eudora Swann and Jed would get along famously, Clay decided, wishing he could introduce them. And were the halfling a few years older, he would make an ideal match for Livvy Childe. The pair of them could talk each other insensible.

There were a few books among the other items in the boxes he had searched, and Clay suspected most of them were enormously valuable. He'd uncovered leather-bound manuscripts in Latin, gloriously illuminated by monks long centuries ago, and a small quarto of *Hamlet* that surely dated from Shakespeare's time. Perhaps one of the Bard's own company, the King's Men, had scribbled those stage directions in the margins.

In all fairness, he could take the *Hamlet* and an armload of other treasures, sell them, and live like a gentleman for several years. The temptation to do so began to put down roots in his imagination. A fashionable house, his own carriage instead of hired job-coaches, a valet . . .

But in the end, he left the books where he'd found them. He wasn't altogether certain why, except that personal profit somehow cheapened his quest for Francesca's Book.

A collection of poetry was not precisely the Holy Grail, and the man seeking it was at best a knight in dented armor, but he was nonetheless bound on a Quest. He meant to conduct it with purity of heart.

On the other hand, should he fail to locate the Petrarch, he would certainly go back and retrieve that *Hamlet*.

Clay did set aside one large book, filled with drawings and descriptions of exotic plants and flowers discovered on a sixteenth-century voyage around the world, intending it as a gift for his mother. She had always loved flowers and spent most days cultivating her gardens or experimenting with plants in the conservatory.

By late afternoon, the pale winter light fading swiftly and no sign of Petrarch, he dispatched Jed for a brace of candles and cleared a wide space in the drafty room to set it. Then, wearily, he lifted an especially heavy box onto the table, pleased to find it crammed with books.

Most were mathematical treatises of some sort, but there were also gilt-edged volumes written in something he supposed was Arabic, and, at the very bottom, Bibles. A great many Bibles. At least one Marquess of Fallon must have had a spiritual bent.

He'd started to replace the books he'd removed when his eye caught a few gold-stamped letters on the spine of a slender volume trapped sideways between the Bibles and the box.

FRANCESC . . .

Stripping off his glove, he unwedged the book and held it to the light. FRANCESCO PETRARCA. CANZONIERE.

Hands shaking, Clay gently opened the cover and turned the pages to a delicate, beautifully colored illustration of a woman with blond hair standing near the Communion rail of a church. On the opposite page, in the lovely script of a gifted calligrapher, were lines written in Italian.

Era 'l giorno ch'al sol si scoloraro.

Clay had no earthly idea what that meant. As he turned the pages, he found more intricate, breathtaking pictures set opposite more groupings of fourteen lines.

If his faltering efforts at poesy had taught him nothing else, he knew that fourteen lines that rhymed in a pattern meant *sonnet*!

He was whirling around in the narrow space, chortling like the village idiot and clutching the small book to his chest, when Jed reappeared in the doorway with the brace of candles.

"I s-say, milord. You gone queer in the brain box?"

In fact, Clay was happy right down to the marrow in his bones. He felt a joy so unaccustomed that he might have flown, had the ceiling been higher or the windows open.

Pleasure and happiness are wholly different things, he realized with sudden clarity of vision. He'd experienced a great deal of the former, and little if any of the latter, until this very moment. He was also damnably dizzy from spinning around in tight circles.

The room stopped whirling a minute or two after he did. And when his gaze fell on the boxes yet to be searched, he experienced an acute shot of panic.

What if this *wasn't* Francesca's Book? What if the real thing still lay hidden under a clutter of porcelain cow creamers and Latin sermons?

Clay resolved to see his Quest through to the very end, just in case. By candlelight he opened every last box and searched all the furniture drawers before turning to Jed with an exhausted smile. "We are done," he said.

Since the grinning, spinning episode, the boy had

kept a careful distance. But he ventured closer when Clay held out a golden guinea.

"This is yours," Clay said, "after you tell the stableman to saddle my horse, and on your promise to return the paintings to this room and see it is left in good order. Agreed?"

Eyes rounder than dinner plates, Jed nodded and scurried off.

Clay reclaimed the books he'd selected in the library, scrawled a note to Fallon sealing the settlement of the gaming debt, and tossed the guinea to Jed when they met in the foyer.

The youngster produced a creditable bow. "You ain't like the others what come here, sir. I hopes you comes back soon."

Clay found another guinea and handed it over. "Thank you for your help, Master Jed. But if all goes well, I won't ever set foot at Wolvercote, or any place like it, again. Wish me luck."

"You bet, guv!" Jed called as Clay headed for the stable. "I means to pray fer you, too."

At midnight, so fatigued he could scarcely turn the key in the lock, Clay opened the door to his London flat and saw that Jed's prayers had fallen on the ears of a deaf deity.

Directly in front of him, lounging in the chair behind his writing table, was the Earl of Montford.

"You live like a pig," he said affably.

Clay closed the door behind him and leaned against it for support. "Greetings, Father. Welcome to the sty. Dare I ask how you got in?"

"A foolish question. By now you should realize I am invariably admitted wherever I choose to go. Have you been sleeping in those clothes?"

"As it happens, yes. On the rare occasions I slept

128

at all. And before you point it out, I have not shaved for three—or is it four?—days."

"Fallon would not provide you so much as a razor?"

Clay was unsurprised his father knew where he had been. If he wished, Montford could probably ferret out how often and in what locations Prinny had used a chamber pot this past week.

"A man with care to his health touches few things at Wolvercote," he said, figuring Montford would come to the point eventually.

"As it happens," Montford said, "I was called to London on a matter of some urgency by the Foreign Office. But the business was concluded more quickly than expected, freeing me to set off for home tomorrow morning. I stopped by to leave you a message, but how fortunate you chanced to arrive while I am here to tell you the news in person."

"Yes indeed," Clay said between his teeth.

"While searching through the rubble on this table," the earl remarked placidly, "I couldn't help noticing that you have been trying your hand at a sonnet." He lifted a scrap of paper. " 'Black-haired lady, wondrous fair—' "

"Enough!" Clay stalked to the desk and snatched the paper from his hand. "This is none of your concern."

"You relieve my mind. There is far too much bad poetry floating about without you adding to the flotsam and jetsam. But scribble away if you must. Perhaps it will keep you out of trouble for a few hours." He focused on the books Clay held against his chest. "Ah, I apprehend that you are *reading*, too. And they say the world holds no surprises. May I see which authors have wrought this miraculous transformation?"

Since Francesca's Book was nestled snugly in the breast pocket of his coat, Clay willingly dropped the others on the table.

Montford briefly examined each one. "Hmmm. Petrarch. Petrarch. More Petrarch. Petrarch yet again. And what have we here. Plants?"

"A gift for Mother," Clay said levelly. "Would you consider delivering it for me?"

"Certainly." He turned a few pages. "I suppose this will please her. Of late, Lady Montford exists only to grub about in the dirt."

Because she prefers the company of snails and slugs to her husband, Clay wanted to say. But he only shrugged and began to pull off his greatcoat.

Montford made a sweeping gesture. "Speaking of dirt, how came you to move from Jermyn Street into this squalid flat? The landlord assures me you have resided here for several months. Since long before I cut off your allowance."

"Have you forgot?" Clay gave him a chilly smile. "I meant to buy into the army, and the money saved on rent was put aside for uniforms and equipment. It was never my intention to remain here beyond a few weeks. By rights, I should even now be on the Peninsula."

"Buried somewhere *in* the Peninsula, more likely. Be sure that Wellington has little use for aristocratic cannon fodder. But let us not pluck that crow again." Montford stood, the book of plants in his hand, and crossed to the door. "I shall remove myself before your body odor causes me to lose my supper. And on the way out, I'll direct your landlord to send up a bath . . . at my expense."

Clay rubbed the back of his neck. "You still haven't told me why you came here in the first place."

"My lamentable memory. Naturally I wished to convey my paternal regards and advise you of my return to Montford House. You were bound to learn I'd come to London. But the coast, as they say, is now clear again."

Just before entering the passageway, Montford paused. "One more thing, Clayburn. I have advised my solicitor to release the rest of your commission money, which you may claim at your convenience."

Minutes later, Clay was still staring at the closed door, trying to make sense of what had just occurred. Something of significance, he was fairly certain, although his brain functioned with the precision of a stomped-on watch.

While he disrobed, and all through the hot soaking bath, he worried at the mystery. By usual standards, Montford had been almost friendly. His gibes seemed more habitual than malicious. And for no discernible reason, he had returned the commission money!

Clay knew better than to assume this unexpected largesse sprang from the goodness of his father's heart. Nor was it sudden remorse after noting the lowly state in which his son was forced to live. Reducing him to penury had been Montford's intention from the start, after all, another ploy to force a marriage with the Albatross.

Had he suddenly changed tactics? Set himself to win by other means what he had failed to achieve by tyranny? Clay rubbed soap through his matted hair. Well, whatever the earl had in mind, it would come to nothing.

His son was no longer the aimless, unsettled man he had been. By the grace of God, Clay thought with a soundless prayer of gratitude, he had met Francesca. He had fallen in love and set a new course for his life. Not a smooth one, for the goddess would not easily be convinced to accept him. To the contrary. But for once, he knew where he was going and what he had to do. Montford was now wholly irrelevant.

Even so, Clay had an eerie sensation that he was missing something vital. That his father, and even

Francesca, harbored a secret he ought to know. Nonsensical, of course, since the two of them had never met.

But as he rinsed his hair in the lukewarm water, he felt very much like the only actor in a play who had not read the entire script.

Chapter 12

Therefore, when flint and iron wear away,
Verse is immortal and shall ne'er decay.
—*Christopher Marlowe*

Whistling cheerfully, Clay guided his horse in and out of the bustling traffic on Piccadilly, on his way at last to Grosvenor Square.

He spotted a flower seller just ahead and pulled over to the curb, but the bouquets, all set in rusty buckets, were unworthy of his goddess. Better to stop off at a reputable florist and order up an elaborate display of hothouse blooms, he decided. Tipping his hat to the disappointed woman, he shook his head. "Perhaps another time, ma'am."

"Well, what der you 'spect, Mr. High 'n' Mighty?" She spat on the pavement. "It's bloody *winter*!"

"So it is." He changed his mind about the fashionable florist. A man in love with the world ought to share his joy with those who most needed it. "I'll have your finest," he said, pressing a guinea into her extended palm.

"For this, you kin take 'em all." She gave him a coy smile. "And me besides, you bein' such a fine-lookin' cove."

He laughed. "You flatter me, my dear. But as I am on my way to meet the lady of my heart, your flowers will have to do."

She passed up a bunch of slightly wilted blossoms

wrapped in a sheet of wet newspaper, which immediately began to drip on his pristine breeches. Well, what were handkerchiefs for but to mop up, he thought, proceeding to do so. Today, nothing could spoil his good mood. With a wave at the flower seller, the bouquet held at arm's length over the street, he continued toward his destination.

Francesca was beginning to thaw, he was reasonably certain, although he'd only his instincts to go on. Naturally she felt compelled to hold him at bay, even when he returned to the inn with her precious Livvy in tow. Her pride demanded resistance. A woman who began so very much set against him would not quickly admit that she had changed her mind.

Fortunately, he was a patient man. And for such a prize he would climb mountains, swim cold rivers, and even restrain his increasingly painful desire for her until she was ready to match it. Did a woman's body actually hurt for a man, he wondered, the way his body ached to make love to Francesca? He should have asked Eudora that question.

The slim volume of Petrarch, nestled securely in the breast pocket of his coat, burned against his heart like a glowing coal. He could scarcely wait to put it in Francesca's hands. Her dark, liquid eyes would shine with pleasure, and perhaps she would thank him with another hug. Maybe even a kiss this time.

Lord, he had been fantasizing about this moment since first clapping eyes on the book. After falling exhausted into his bed last night, he had dreamed of all the ways she would thank him.

What would she think if he asked her to marry him?

He wanted to. He'd rehearsed a proposal on his ride from Wolvercote to London. But now he couldn't remember the words, and besides, she was a long way from ready to accept his offer. Beginning to thaw was not the same as melting. He must be patient awhile more.

And, too, his poem was nowhere near finished. So far he had little more than a mishmash of badly mangled rhymes and a title—"Sonnet to a Goddess." "Ode to a Goddess" sounded better, but he wasn't precisely sure what an ode was. Better stick to a plain old sonnet, he told himself. Odes were probably a devilish sight longer.

Clay dismounted in front of Francesca's town house and tossed the reins to one of the boys who darted from the shrubbery of the Grosvenor Square garden. His heart overflowing with goodwill, he found coins for each of the other boys, too.

Later, he meant to visit Montford's solicitor and pocket the rest of his commission money, after which he would dispense a large portion of it to flower sellers, street urchins, and church poor boxes. A lucky man should spread his good fortune around.

But moments later, his luck screeched to a halt. Firmly blocking the door, Francesca's peevish butler announced that she was not at home.

At first, Clay didn't believe him. Then a more appalling possibility iced down his spine. Could she have given instructions that he was not to be admitted? Until that instant, it had not occurred to him that she would turn him away. But the more he thought on it, the more likely it seemed.

She feared him. Or rather, she feared the way she responded to him. He'd enough experience to recognize physical attraction when he saw it in a woman's eyes and in the small female gestures that expressed more clearly than words what she was feeling.

Francesca wanted him. She might not wholly realize it yet, or she might be unready to admit it, but she wanted him. And either way, her first reaction would be to throw up defenses.

That's what he figured anyway, as the butler stared at him with disdain. At bottom, he hadn't a clue to Francesca's thoughts or feelings, which only meant he had to persist long enough to decipher them. For certain, he would not easily be turned from her door.

"Naturally, I wish to leave a message," he said with all the aristocratic hauteur bred into him through six centuries of Montford earls. "You may show me into a parlor and supply paper, pen, and ink."

The butler retreated a step, his hand still firmly clamped on the door. From his belligerent scowl, he was more than ready to slam it in Clay's face, but something distracted him. He glanced over his shoulder.

"Who is it, Peters?"

Clay recognized Ann's voice. "It's Clayburn," he said loudly enough to be heard over Peters's mumbled response. "There appears to be some misunderstanding."

"Oh, dear. Please come in, my lord."

Stalking past the butler, he bowed to Ann. "I see you have made your way home from the Black Dove without coming to harm."

"My, yes. Jer—Mr. Porter was most solicitous. He took care of everything. And we are all very grateful to you, too, my lord." A faint smile curved her lips. "Well, perhaps Livvy is not."

"I daresay." He grinned back. "Is Miss Francesca Childe at home this morning? I wish to pay my regards."

"She will be sorry to have missed you. But Mrs. Beaton swept her off nearly two hours ago, and I understand they will be gone for most of the day." She glanced at the flowers he was holding. "May I take those from you and have them put in water?"

"Oh, your butler can see to that." He shoved the dripping wad of newspaper and stems into the outraged servant's hand.

At the same time, a young man thundered down the stairs. "*There* you are, Peters. I've been ringing for you forever! We need you to summon a hack." Belatedly he noticed the other two people standing in the foyer. "Sorry, Ann. And you, sir. We're in something of a hurry."

"We?" Ann inquired with unaccustomed sternness. "If *we* includes Livvy, think again. You know she is forbidden to leave the house without Cesca's permission."

"But Cesca's not here! And we meant to ask her this morning, but she was gone before we even woke up."

Bemused, Clay took the boy's measure. Blond and slender, he was obviously another whelp of Bromley Childe, perhaps a year or two older than the twins. And clearly he had lamentable ambitions to join the dandy set. Over a vile yellow waistcoat, those high shirt-points and overwrought cravat would have strangled any but the most determined young man trying to make a splash in London.

"Nevertheless," Ann replied, "Livvy cannot go with you."

"And who are *you* to say?" the boy demanded. "In Father's absence, *I* am the man of the family. And what harm can she come to in my company? Even Cesca would agree with that."

Not likely, Clay thought, wondering what they had planned for the afternoon. He suspected Livvy had cozened her brother into another of her disreputable schemes to go where proper young ladies never went.

"Arthur, do be quiet for a moment and recall your manners. Have you failed to notice we have a guest?" Ann gave Clay an apologetic smile. "My lord, may I introduce my brother, Arthur Childe? He has just come down from Oxford to stay with us. Arthur, make your bow to Lord Clayburn."

"Clayburn?" The boy's mouth dropped. "The *famous* Lord Clayburn? I say, what a stroke of luck. Pleased to meet you!" After a moment, he remembered to bow. "I'm at Magdalen, too, my lord. Everybody still talks of you there. Practically a legend you are, what with the sheep in the chapel and the two dox—er, ladies you smuggled into the don's room, and—"

"Never mind," Clay broke in. "Your sister will not care to hear of my youthful transgressions." He extended his hand, which was pumped vigorously by the enthusiastic Arthur. "A pleasure to meet you, too, Mr. Childe. I hope you don't mean to wrench my arm from the socket so early in our acquaintance."

Flushing brightly, the boy let go and clasped his hands behind his back. "Sorry, my lord. And please call me Arthur."

"Very well, Arthur." With dismay, Clay recognized a woeful case of hero worship. For all the wrong reasons, of course, not that there were any right reasons to venerate a rakehell. "I am not partial to formality either," he said, unsure how to deal with Francesca's cousin. One day soon, he hoped, they would be related. But for now, given Arthur's awestruck regard, he was loath to encourage familiarity. "Should we chance to meet again," he temporized, "address me as Clayburn. Or sir."

"I shall indeed, Clayburn. Sir."

"*Oh!* It's *you!*"

Everyone's attention turned to Livvy, whose precipitous rush down the staircase had come to a halt when she spied Clayburn.

He almost laughed at the look of frustration on her pretty face. Poor Livvy. The Fates were cruel indeed to have led him there minutes before she made her escape.

Gathering her cloak around her, she completed her descent to the foyer with a show of imperious disdain. Even Clay was impressed. Willful girl. Like ignited flash powder, she would not be contained.

"We are going to a balloon ascent," she proclaimed as if issuing an edict. "Arthur, have you secured a hackney? Do so at once, or we'll be late to arrive."

"And who has been waiting an eternity for you to trick yourself out?" Arthur responded with indignation. "I'm not the one who's been primping in front of a mirror since the world was created."

"Then why is your dressing-room floor littered with neckcloths?" she retorted. "I went there first in search of you. Obviously a typhoon swept through. That, or you were making a futile effort to—"

Clay closed his ears to their squabble, wondering if he dared intervene. Any protest Ann might make would be ineffectual, he knew. If Livvy were to be stopped, he would have to do it. But how? Short of wrestling her to the floor, what *could* he do?

Most important, what would Francesca want him to do?

"A balloon ascent?" he asked just as Livvy lunged, hands extended, for her brother's throat. "How diverting. It's been years since I saw one. Do you mind if I accompany you, Arthur?"

Shoving Livvy away, Arthur turned to him with shining eyes. "Oh, please do, sir. It's to be a race, you know. And Lord Heston has promised to take us up in his carriage. We'll follow the balloons and try to get to the first one that lands before any of the other—"

"Shut up, you ninny!" Livvy snapped. "Lord Clayburn has better things to do than chase a balloon."

She was right about that, he thought. But now

that he knew Heston was tangled up in this, he had no choice.

"What could be more fun?" Arthur insisted. "Besides, he's already said he wants to come with us. And I should like that above all things."

"I wouldn't!" Livvy shot back.

"But then," Clay told her implacably, "I would be compelled to remain here for the afternoon and make sure you did the same. Ann has said that you are forbidden to leave the house without supervision, Livvy. And for all that he is your older brother and a man of obvious savoir faire, Arthur is new to London. He does not know his way around so well as I." He turned to the wide-eyed youngster. "Am I mistaken?"

"Oh, no, sir. Fact is, I don't even know the way to Hyde Park."

"The hackney driver will get us there!" Livvy glared at Clay. "We'll do well enough on our own."

"No doubt," he agreed. "But even so, I'll trail along on my horse to keep you company. Ann, if Miss Francesca returns before we do, please assure her the situation is well in hand. Or do you wish to come with us?"

"I—no," she replied, a blush stealing over her cheeks. "Mr. Porter has promised to call, you see."

"Excellent." He smiled at her, and then at Arthur. "Shall we be off?"

Chapter 13

The passion you pretended
was only to obtain.
—*John Dryden*

Seated at a table in the dining room of the Crillon Hotel, Francesca absently rendered a scone to crumbs between her fingers while Maria Beaton, ignoring her companion's lack of attention, summarized the accomplishments of their frenzied morning together.

A lost cause, Francesca thought at the corners of her mind. What did it all matter?

At least she had been honest about her feelings. When they set out four hours ago, she had stated quite frankly that she'd rather mount a charge against Boney's Imperial Guard than contend with the arrangements for a lavish ball. And it didn't help that Ann and Livvy displayed even less interest in what was supposed to be their evening of triumph. Along the way, they had lost their initial enthusiasm for the ball or directed it elsewhere.

But Maria had been determined to proceed. "*I* shall handle all the details," she'd insisted "You have only to make decisions and cease worrying about the girls. They are certain to come about."

The morning had passed in a blur of flowers and cards and print styles, while Francesca's thoughts perversely wandered to the man she had vowed not to think about. What in blazes had become of him?

It seemed an eternity since Clayburn had left her at

the Black Dove. Could he still be at Wolvercote after all this time, tossing dice with the other reprobates? Some of them had already returned to London, she knew, for she'd caught Livvy flirting with Lord Heston at Lady Potsworth's rout last night.

Finally, after hours of consulting with printers for the invitations, an agency to supply extra staff, several obsequious florists, and the manager of a small orchestra currently favored by Society hostesses, she had declared herself unable to continue without an infusion of strong tea.

And still Lord Clayburn haunted her, as if he had taken up residence in her head. Sometimes she felt him moving about her body, exploring, evaluating, leaving his mark.

"Francesca?" Maria tapped her spoon against the teapot. "Where have you gone?"

Her head shot up. "I'm so sorry. What were you saying?"

"Nothing of importance. But I sense you have something on your mind. Do you wish to discuss it with me?"

"No. Thank you. That is, I could not." Nervously, Francesca rolled a currant from the scone between her thumb and forefinger. "Have you ever taken a lover?" she blurted, to her own considerable astonishment.

"Oh, certainly," Maria replied easily. "Several, in fact, Mr. Beaton having considerably cocked up his toes within two years of our ill-advised marriage. Why do you ask?"

Heat stung Francesca's cheeks. "Oh my. I beg you to pardon me, Maria. That was an insufferably rude question."

"Not at all. I am convinced you inquire for reasons of your own, and not from curiosity about my personal affairs. Are you by chance considering a lover for yourself? Clayburn, perhaps?"

Francesca longed to slide under the table. Or better, into the Thames. However had Maria guessed? "Of course not. I s-scarcely know him." The lies felt like hot coals in her throat. "The very idea would be insupportable, given my circumstances and inclinations. But . . . I just wondered . . ." Her voice burned away.

Maria made a *tsk*ing noise. "All that Italian passion coursing through your veins, and you a virgin at one-and-thirty! It is positively unnatural, my dear." She spooned honey into her tea. "May I offer a bit of unsolicited advice? Clayburn is a gentleman, for all his scandalous reputation, and I've never known him to seduce an innocent. If you want him for yourself— and I suspect you do—you must make your interest very clear."

"I have *never* said I want him," Francesca returned defensively. "Nor any other man, for that matter. And if ever I thought to fancy Lord Clayburn, I would soon think better of it. He is a degenerate goat." The much-maligned currant was squashed messily between her fingers.

"Oh, never a *goat*!" Maria laughed. "More like an unbroken stallion, and what a pity 'twould be to clap a bit in his mouth. Clayburn is much more fascinating as he is, sulky, defiant, and unpredictable. The woman who draws him to her bed and keeps him there past a fortnight will be fortunate indeed."

Licking crumbs from her fingers, Francesca wondered how all that could be accomplished.

"He is not my sort, of course," Maria continued reflectively. "My present lover is almost his exact age, although not nearly so handsome. But then, few men are." She took a sip of tea. "I speak out of turn, Francesca, and you must not take lessons from me.

143

As a widow of independent means, I am able to do as I like, so long as I remain discreet. And because I care most for my writing, my female friends, and my causes, the men I select are compelled to remain in the background of my affections."

"Toys," Francesca said, repressing her disgust.

"By their choice, you may be sure. I am far too preoccupied with other matters to seek a man or cater to him. Men come to me for reasons of their own and generally stay for a considerable time." She reached for a jam tart. "You will, and should, expect more from your lovers, in the event you decide not to marry. But I believe you ought to set your sights high and demand the very best. You can have it, my dear, with a snap of your fingers."

Wishing she had never embarked on this conversation, Francesca could not stop herself from continuing it. "What precisely *is* the very best?" she asked curiously.

"Why, a love match with a handsome, intelligent, faithful husband. He must have a sense of humor, for that is essential if you are to live together for very long. And he must equal you in passion, which will be a considerable challenge for any man. Naturally he must possess a tolerant nature, if he is to endure your frequent bouts of temper."

"And I can have all that with a snap of my fingers?" Francesca erupted in laughter, snapping away to no avail. "As you see, this paragon has failed to appear. But never mind, for I cannot believe that such a man exists. And if he does, he is even now courting a younger, more pliable bride."

"Well, perhaps you are right to be skeptical, my dear. Such a love as I would hope for you is rare indeed."

"Yes, it is, and I'll not waste a single moment indulging implausible fantasies. But even a passing affair is out of the question, should I have such a notion. Anything I do must reflect on Ann and Livvy, and I am in London solely on their behalf." She released a small sigh. "And you know, Maria, my father is very ill. Above all things, I wish to return home as soon as possible."

"It does credit to you." Maria took her hand. "For now, you are pushed and pulled from all directions. But circumstances will change, as they always do, so you must not burn any proverbial bridges just yet."

"Oh my." Francesca folded her napkin and set it on the table. "This is a decidedly improper conversation, and we are scandalizing the good ladies at the table next to us. But I promise not to ignite a single bridge I may later wish to cross."

"What think you of a brisk walk?" Maria asked, standing with a groan. "I must do something to counter those three cream-filled pastries, not to mention that enormous jam tart."

After settling the bill, they strolled at a snail's pace toward Hyde Park. The pavement was clogged with pedestrians, and a veritable parade of vehicles crammed the street, every one of them aimed in the same direction.

"How odd," Maria said. " 'Tis only two o'clock. Not at all the fashionable hour to promenade."

Francesca stumbled as a young buck brushed against her shoulder on the way past, obviously in a hurry. Finally they turned onto Park Lane and saw people rushing from every direction toward a large crowd that had gathered in a wide circle on the open field. From this distance, she could not make out what had caught their attention.

Carriages and gigs lined Park Lane on both sides, forcing any traffic proceeding elsewhere to weave in and out with a great deal of shouting and cursing from the drivers.

Maria plucked at her sleeve. "Shall we make our escape while we can, or do you wish to see what this commotion is about?"

"The commotion, please." In all her years, Francesca had never seen so many people in one place. She doubted the entire county of Rutlandshire could assemble a congregation of this size.

"Very well, then. Stay close by and we'll go around the long way. I know a spot where we may have an excellent view."

Ten minutes later, they came to a small rise midway between the line of carriages and the noisy mob. A few others had also discovered the vantage point, but Francesca and Maria found a clear patch beneath the bare branches of a tree.

"I wish I'd thought to bring my opera glasses," Maria said, opening her parasol. "Can you see anything, my dear?"

A full seven inches taller than her friend, Francesca stood on tiptoe and made out two splotches of bright color against the brown grass in the center of the crowd. "I'm not altogether certain, but I think we are to witness a balloon ascent. How wonderful! I have longed to see one."

Maria was less enthralled. "In my experience, it means a long period of tedium followed by a few moments of breathtaking beauty. Then the balloon is gone from sight, and one is like to be trampled by the multitudes leaving the park."

Francesca remembered her manners. "Perhaps we should go, then, before the stampede."

"Nonsense. I shall occupy myself with the essay I mean to write this evening, and you will advise me when the balloons are aloft. Enjoy yourself, my dear, but do not wander away."

For half an hour Francesca delighted in the colorful spectacle. Jugglers and organ-grinders with monkeys entertained at the edges of the crowd. Children laughed and squealed. The cries of hawkers flogging oranges, gingerbread, and cheese pies rose above the general clamor.

No balloons rose, however. She was fairly certain there were two of them, both giving the aeronauts difficulty of some sort. Now and again, a raucous voice demanded they get on about it.

She wondered how the balloons were to be inflated, but Maria's eyes had the slightly glazed look of intense concentration, and Francesca knew better than to interrupt. Instead, she turned her attention to the vehicles lined up along Park Lane.

Only men occupied the carriages or strode among them to greet friends. Strange, that. On the field below her, there was no shortage of female observers. One more thing about London Society she failed to understand, she reflected with a sigh.

Just then, amid the dark blue and brown coats, she caught a glimpse of pink. Shading her eyes with a hand, she tried to find it again. Sure enough, a lone female in a straw bonnet tied with a wide pink ribbon was perched on the driver's bench of an open barouche, seated next to a gentleman wearing a tall hat. Behind them, four or five men crowded the passenger squabs.

Curious, she watched the small party for a time, wondering why only one woman had been admitted to such exclusively male company. Something about the way she moved seemed familiar, although the barouche was too far away for Francesca to identify her.

Suddenly the woman pulled off her bonnet with a

flourish, revealing short blond curls. And when she tossed her head, Francesca knew there could be no mistake.

"Livvy." The word came out in a growl.

"I beg your pardon?" Maria said.

Francesca was almost too furious to respond. She jabbed her finger toward the barouche. "Look there."

"Oh. I see," Maria acknowledged after a moment. "That is Lord Heston beside her, and Clarence Briggs is among the passengers, along with a pair of other wastrels. I do not recognize the fifth man."

With a fairly good idea who that fifth man was, Francesca charged across the grass with Maria at her heels.

Despite her shorter legs, Maria caught up and seized her elbow, yanking her to a halt. "Take a deep breath, young woman, and calm yourself. You do not wish to make a scene."

Homicide was more what she had in mind. But Francesca obediently drew in several long, soothing drafts of air and counted from one to ten. The hot blaze of her temper settled into a jittery fire.

"How am I to detach that insufferable girl *without* a scene?" she asked as they proceeded more sedately toward Park Lane. For the first time, she noticed an enormous black gelding tied up behind the barouche. She was almost certain she had seen that horse before.

Arthur spotted her then, jumping up so quickly he made the carriage rock. "Cesca!" he called, waving his hat. "Over here. It's me."

And you are a dead man, she thought, carving a grim smile on her face as she glanced up at Livvy.

Eyes rounder than blue Wedgwood saucers, the miscreant slid closer to Lord Heston and lifted her pert chin defiantly.

It would take heavy artillery to dislodge her, Francesca knew, still smiling as she came up to Arthur. "How serendipitous to find you in all this crowd," she said, watching him struggle to decipher *serendipitous*.

He soon gave up. "I call it lucky," he said. "Maybe that means my luck will hold for the race. No telling which way the balloons will go, but we'll beat the others to where they land. Heston is a prime whip."

It was Francesca's turn to decipher. "The balloons are racing?"

"Didn't I just say so? First one to touch ground twenty miles from here in any direction wins. But nobody cares about that. We are wagering which driver arrives ahead of the others and shakes hands with a balloonist. That's why all these coaches are lined up here, silly. When the balloons take off, so do we."

"Rather like a fox hunt," said a deep baritone voice just behind her, "the fox being irrelevant. All the fun is in the chase."

Francesca spun around to face Lord Clayburn. *His* horse! The one he had ridden when they set out for Wolvercote. She ought to have recognized it immediately. And guessed he would be at the bottom of this quagmire. "How dare you?" she whispered savagely.

Before she could object, he slipped a firm hand around her elbow and steered her away from the barouche. "In private," he warned. "The street is no place to have one of your temper tantrums." Drawing her to a stop within sight of the crowd, but distant enough to permit conversation without fear of an audience, he let go of her and bowed. "You may proceed now."

"How dare you?" she repeated, wanting to pummel him. "This is monstrous! I cannot fathom your intentions, Clayburn. You exert yourself to save Livvy from utter ruin, only to throw her back to the wolves."

"Are you quite finished?" he inquired when she ran out of breath.

"No!" Defiantly she loaded up another barrage of insults and fired them off. "You are beyond contempt. A devious, manipulative, self-serving beast. Pond scum. A snake in the woods."

"Grass." He looked amused. "A snake in the *grass*."

"A viper is a viper, wherever it slithers. And do not think to dupe me again with pitiful excuses for your behavior, because I know better than to believe a single word you say. Be sure of that, sir. I know precisely why you lie to me and to what ends you will go, though why you persist defies all reason."

His eyes glittered in the sunlight. "Except that you are speaking precious little sense, Miss Childe, I have never in my life been so enchanted. And although you fling bolts of lightning at my head, I believe I would sell my soul to the devil at this very moment for one kiss. From *you*, I hasten to add. Not a kiss from the devil."

"Poppycock! You *are* the devil, Clayburn."

"On occasion. But in the last two hours I have become something far more terrifying to my own sensibilities—a hovering nursemaid. Do you care to hear how that came about, or would you prefer to continue scolding me?"

"Oh, the former, please. I promise to remain civil and mute." After all, she could throttle him later.

His teasing grin warmed into a smile. "Ah, I have missed you, termagant. My recent incarceration at Wolvercote may have lasted only a few days, but it felt very much like eternal damnation."

"You ought to know."

"Witch. When I called on you this morning, only to learn that you had already gone out, I chanced to encounter Livvy and Master Arthur. They were in a considerable hurry to leave, but Arthur recognized my name when we were introduced and stopped long enough to make my acquaintance. Who would have thought I'd become something of a legend among the Oxford underclassmen? He thinks me a regular out-and-outer and a great gun, you will be astonished to hear."

"Not at all. You are notorious on several continents, and he is a nodcock."

Clayburn laughed. "Although Livvy tried her best to shut him off, Arthur could not resist blathering their plans for the afternoon. He is, as you observed, in high spirits about this race. It was when he confided that the dashing Lord Heston had invited them into his carriage that I was thrust willy-nilly into the role of chaperon."

"Hah!"

"Yes, I do understand. A woeful example of miscasting. But needs must when the devil drives, and what with Lord Heston playing the devil in this particular farce, I *very* reluctantly took on the part of bear-leader."

"Why did you not stop them from leaving the house at all?" she demanded. Irrationally, she knew, for how could he do so short of tackling them in the foyer and locking them in the cellars?

Clayburn looked pained. "Arthur believes his father is to join the party, although I rather doubt that will come to pass. Haring about the countryside in an open carriage is scarcely Bromley's notion of a good time."

"So you mean to hare in his place? Oh, that will certainly help!" Francesca shook her head vigorously. "How can adding yet another blackguard to this scandalbroth serve any purpose?"

"I quite agree. But you needn't imagine I have the

slightest influence in this matter, for good *or* ill. Livvy drives daggers into my chest each time she looks at me, and I am the last man on earth Heston would oblige. Thus far, I have used young Arthur's misplaced hero worship as an excuse to hang about where I am otherwise de trop, in hopes the balloons fail to go up, which often happens."

"Well, I am not so chickenhearted as you," she declared. "Livvy and Arthur will come home with me if I am forced to drag them by the scruffs of their necks."

"A delightful picture, to be sure. Caricatures will be hung in every shop window—'Tigress and Her Cubs.' "

"Oh."

A wave of bewildered frustration, like the ones that had swept over her almost hourly since leaving Rutlandshire, left her speechless. She put a wrong foot wherever she stepped, and London outwitted her at every turn. She had even ripped into Lord Clayburn, who had stood her friend once and seemed ready to do so again.

She ought to be grateful. Assuredly she owed him an apology for her blast of temper. But she also understood his motives, which were wholly selfish and deplorable. Resentment clouded her every thought and feeling about this man. If she scorned the kindnesses he did for her, it was because she scorned the reasons for them.

And, truth be told, she feared her own vulnerability to his charm. When all that focused male sensuality was directed straight at her, her insides promptly turned to mush. Meantime, some other creature that looked like her on the outside went on fighting him.

A small shock raced from her fingertips all the way to her toes. Looking down, she realized he had taken hold of her hands. Through his heavy leather riding gloves and her butter-soft kidskin gloves, she felt the slight tension in his grip and the rhythmic pulse in his veins, slower than hers and far steadier.

"You must not worry so much," he said gently. "Some matters are beyond your control, specifically those to do with Livvy, who is beyond *anyone's* control."

"Bromley told me the same thing," she admitted, forcing her disordered mind from Clayburn to the problem at hand. "But I cannot believe she will toss away her entire future for a few reckless hours of excitement."

"At heart she is a gambler, you know. And gamesters must risk all to feel alive. They ruin themselves and their families to recapture the brief, mad rush they experienced at their first big win. The thrill nearly always eludes them thereafter, but they will not be stopped."

"How does this signify?" she protested weakly. "Livvy has never won so much as a farthing at cards or dice."

His thumbs began to make small circles in the palms of her hands. "Ah, but Livvy plays a different sort of game. Some men, and women, too, are addicted to sexual pleasure. Others pursue intoxication by eating opium. Power, fame, even artistic creativity, can enslave people beyond reason. And once chained by their own compulsions, few make the considerable effort it would require to escape. It is the way of the world."

Remember this, Francesca told herself stonily. The next time you imagine that Clayburn will ever become other than the rakehell he has always been, *remember*. This once, he is speaking the truth about himself.

"I understand," she said, removing her hands from his as a bone-numbing chill swept through her. All around her, colors faded to shades of black and gray. She looked past Clayburn, over a dingy field of shadow puppets to a charcoal-colored balloon that must have begun to inflate because it was clearly visible above the crowd. Then it collapsed, and the crowd groaned in chorus.

She forced her knees to straighten and willed a javelin into her spine. "Advise me, sir. Am I to simply abandon Arthur and Livvy to those spiders?"

"Be easy. I expect Maria Beaton has already devised a plan to separate Livvy from the coach, and we have only to take our cues from her. As for Arthur, you must calmly wave him good-bye, for he means to follow those balloons. The race presents no danger, I assure you. Heston is an excellent driver, and even that job-house vehicle is safe enough while he holds the reins."

"You fail to reassure me."

"Nor will I fob you off with equivocations. Truth be told, Arthur is in for a wild ride tonight." Clayburn moved to her side and took her arm, which she had forgotten to stiffen. "For now, shall we concentrate on Livvy? Please take no insult, but you can best help by saying nothing at all."

Offended, primarily because he was right, she allowed him to escort her back to the carriage.

Maria, engaged in a lively conversation with Lord Heston, must have possessed eyes in the back of her head. Without turning, she beckoned Francesca to her side. "Is it not grossly unfair, my dear? These gentlemen will soon chase the very wind itself, leaving us behind to choke on their dust."

Treason! Francesca's hands clenched and unclenched, but she smiled and nodded politely.

"I have offered to take you up, Mrs. Beaton," Heston

said, gesturing with his whip. "There is room for one more in the carriage."

"Oh, were it only possible!" Maria heaved a dramatic sigh. "But I have other commitments for this evening, and a lady must honor her commitments. I daresay Olivia regrets that she, too, must stay behind after the balloons are launched, having accepted an invitation to Lady Felterpell's party. Is that not correct, Francesca?"

Francesca nodded again, furious with herself for misjudging her friend's intentions. When would she ever stop leaping to false conclusions? From childhood, that had been her besetting sin.

"I'm not going to that silly party," Livvy declared, crinkling her nose at the very idea of Lady Felterpell. "Nobody will miss me. And all the men of consequence are joining the race."

"Perhaps I have mistaken the situation," Maria said thoughtfully. "Surely you can all return in time for Lady Felterpell's drum. Indeed, if Lord Heston promises to bring you back by seven o'clock, I see no reason for you not to enjoy this adventure."

No reason? Anger mounting inside her again, Francesca chewed at her tongue to keep it under control.

With a frown, Heston glanced at his companions, who looked horrified at the suggestion of a deadline. Clearly they anticipated quite a different sort of evening. "In fact," he said, "there is very little chance we'll make our way to London again before tomorrow's breakfast. I am sorry for it, Livvy, but without question you must return home in company with Miss Childe."

"I won't! You said I could go with you! You *promised*."

"Nothing of the sort," he said tightly. "You cozened your father to play escort, but he appears to

155

have thought better of it. Without his company, you cannot—"

"My brother is here! Arthur can be my escort." Midstream, she changed tactics. "Don't you *want* me to come along, Rupert? We'll have such fun."

Francesca watched in disgust as Livvy rubbed her fingers along Heston's forearm. Then, to her astonishment, he seized the wandering hand and gazed sternly at Livvy's startled face.

"You will remain here," he said in a tone that brooked no opposition. "Tomorrow afternoon, or whenever it is convenient, I shall call on you at Grosvenor Square. And if you cease making a fuss now, perhaps I'll even take you up in my curricle. To date, no female has been permitted to drive with me when I put my bays to their paces."

Her mouth a round O, Livvy considered her options. "I want to follow the balloons," she decided.

Heston swung down from the barouche and held out his arms. "That is no longer a choice. *Out*, Olivia. *Now!*"

A few seconds later, Lord Heston handed Livvy over to Francesca. "All yours," he said. Then, turning to the pouting girl, he brushed back a drooping feather on her bonnet. "Wish me luck in the race, Livvy."

She made an indeterminate sound.

For a moment, his gaze caught Francesca's. She detected mutual understanding and a bit of sympathy on his part. How very odd. Yet another rakehell had just exhibited a thread of decency. Not that Lord Heston and Clayburn were remotely alike, beyond their attachment to vice.

She had no idea what to make of all this, except that Livvy had once again been saved from ruin by a man who generally considered any willing female fair game. And no question about it, Livvy was more than willing. She had made that clear in front of witnesses, including her temporary guardian and her own brother. Shameless!

Maria must have seen the fire in her eyes. "Come, my dear," she said to Livvy. "One balloon is already inflated, and the other nearly so. Soon the tether ropes will be loosed, and they'll be off. We'll have a much better view from the embankment." As she drew the girl away, she winked at Francesca.

"That was well done, don't you think?" Clayburn said, moving to her side. "I was certain Maria could deal with the situation."

"She made a good beginning," Francesca acknowledged. "But it was Lord Heston who brought Livvy to heel. I am still amazed at it. What is between them, do you suppose?"

He shrugged. "They are the last two individuals on the planet who concern me, unless they are causing you distress. For now, all is well, so may we forget them for the rest of the afternoon? I most especially wish to be alone with you, Fra—Miss Childe. Perhaps after the balloon ascension? I have something to give you, and—"

"But what of Arthur?" she broke in as her cousin's laugh brayed from the carriage, followed by an oath he ought not have known. "He is only a boy, and in exceedingly bad company. Can we rescue him, too, do you suppose?"

Clayburn's silvery eyes flashed with anger. "You are not the halfling's mother," he said between taut lips. "And should you humiliate him in front of men he is trying to impress, he will not soon forgive you. Trust me on that."

Why was Clayburn so furious of a sudden? All she'd done was show a little concern for Arthur. He was not in her charge, of course, but she could not help but

157

care what became of him. Should he turn himself into another Bromley, the Sotherton title would pass through *two* generations of profligate lackwits. For Papa's sake, she had no choice but to interfere.

"I don't want Arthur to go with those men," she said rigidly. "They will corrupt him. What is worse, he badly wants them to."

"Yes, he does." Clayburn turned her to face him and put his hands on her shoulders. "Young men crave excitement. You have no idea how tedious Oxford can be, especially when every nerve in the body is vibrating with rather primitive urges. Not all of them have to do with women, by the way. And those that do not are the most difficult to explain."

"I quite understand," she said. "You speak of rebellion. I have often felt it in myself. But when a young man's perfectly natural rebellion leads him to drunken oblivion, or to wager which raindrop will first slide to the bottom of the casement, what is the point?"

"There is none, I have belatedly come to realize."

His fingers pressed into the muscles below her nape, rubbing away the tension that had gathered there. All the rest of it was balled up in her stomach. No. Only some. The part relating to Clayburn had formed tight bands around her heart.

When she began to relax, he brought one hand to cradle her chin. "If you happen to ask me, very nicely, I will agree to follow Heston's carriage on horseback and make sure that Arthur doesn't get in over his head."

Her gaze slid away. Once again, Clayburn sought to throw her off balance with an act of kindness. If only she had someone else, *anyone* else, to ask. But there was only this man, and the treacherous current beneath the surface of everything he said and did. She knew exactly where it would carry her, were she so foolish as to trust him for a single instant.

But so long as he stood willing, for transparently selfish reasons, to do her another service, what was the harm in accepting? Purely for Arthur's sake, of course. Swallowing a lump of pride, she tried to appear delighted. "Oh, please do go with him. Although I suppose this means I'll be forced to let you teach me to dance. Wasn't that the agreement? If you did me another favor—"

"Never mind about that. This good deed is free and clear. And truth be told, I so rarely attend balls that I've long since forgot how to dance. No more *deals* between us, Francesca. They are meaningless, like the raindrop wagers you abhor. But I warn you, Arthur has the bit between his teeth. While I probably can keep him out of trouble tonight, what he sees will only whet his appetite for more."

"Th-then what?"

"As it happens, I do have an idea." He brushed her nose with his gloved forefinger. "But it can wait until you call on me again for help, should you elect to do so. I advise you to exhaust all other recourses beforehand."

"That means, I suppose, that your idea is unlikely to meet with my approval."

"You'll downright loathe it," he said with a laugh. "Ah! There go the balloons! I must retrieve my poor horse before the barouche tows him away. Keep your chin up, sweetheart. Arthur will return intact, I promise, if a bit tattered about the edges."

Francesca watched Clayburn lope up the hill with his athletic stride and disappear into the throng of milling traffic. Then she turned her gaze skyward and saw the balloons pass directly over her head. When the men in the wicker gondolas leaned out to wave at the crowd, she found herself waving back excitedly.

All too soon, the enormous balloons were no more than dabs of red and yellow and green against the clear blue sky. How swiftly the breeze caught them up and swept them away, she thought with a pang of envy. And how glorious it would be to loose her hair to the wind and fly in just such a way, with no fetters of propriety or obligations to keep her earthbound.

But, as Bromley liked to say, a chap must play the cards he's dealt. And since women generally found themselves holding deuces and treys, they must play cautiously indeed.

Good heavens, she thought, looking around for Maria and Livvy. She was starting to think like a gamester!

Chapter 14

Doubts are more cruel than the
worst of truths.

—Molière

Wearing a dressing gown and a pair of slippers,
Francesca wandered to a window in her bedchamber
while servants removed the ceramic bathing tub and
lit candles against the winter twilight. As she gazed
outside, the sky slowly darkened to a deep, ashy blue.
Tendrils of mist began to curl around the chimney
pots on nearby roofs.

It would be a foggy night, she thought, wishing she
could curl up with a book and enjoy a few hours of soli-
tude. But Ann was looking forward to Lady Cowper's
ball, because Jeremy Porter had promised to be there,
and Livvy had secret reasons of her own for wearing
her nicest gown.

Since the balloon race, Livvy had been unnaturally
biddable, which Francesca regarded as a sign of trouble
to come. An openly defiant Livvy was far easier to contend with than the sly creature she had become.

When the servants were gone, Francesca took her
brush from the dressing table and knelt on a cushion
by the fire to dry her hair. It would take nearly an
hour, she knew, followed by a long session with the
complaining maidservant. All the pins in England
could not contain her thick, freshly washed hair, and
she really ought to have it shorn.

But that would mean accepting the probability of a

long stay in the city, when she longed for the peace of Sotherton Manor. There, she dried her hair by the hearth in Papa's library while he read to her, and her stomach never roiled with dread of Livvy's next cut-up or Arthur's plunges into the cesspools of London.

Just now, the servants were prying her cousin from his bed, where he had spent nearly all the day-light hours of this past week. He would likely swill several cups of strong coffee, eat all the dry toast his liquor-soaked belly would accept, and apply himself to the matter of dressing for yet another night on the town with Lord Clayburn.

With a stern application of self-discipline, she had thus far refrained from interfering. But for the life of her, she could not make sense of Clayburn's be-nighted plan.

How could an excess of debauchery set Arthur straight again? The formula had certainly failed to work for Bromley and Clayburn, who'd exceeded every excess for many a year. Absolute proof, in her opinion, that men were more apt to embrace a rake-hell life, once begun, than turn away in disgust.

But Clayburn insisted this was the only way to disil-lusion Arthur, and she had no better idea to offer. At times she even found herself wishing that she, too, could experience a week of unbridled revelry, although drinking and gaming were not among the wicked things she imagined herself doing.

Her hair crackled as she stroked the brush, and her face grew painfully warm. Not sure if that was due to the fire or her searing thoughts, she turned on the cushion and applied herself vigorously to the damp tangle curling down her back.

Into which den of iniquity would Clayburn lead her feckless cousin tonight? she wondered. By now the boy must be up to his shirt-points in debt, with no way in creation to honor them. Better if he'd been introduced to vice by his father, who added no tinge of glamour to a life of dissipation. But Bromley had apparently dropped off the face of the earth, leaving Arthur to model himself after the bedazzling Lord Clayburn.

A soft knock at the door brought her to her feet with a start.

"Lord Clayburn has arrived," the butler said, averting his eyes from her dishabille. "I have put him in the Red Saloon."

"Did he ask to speak with me?" she asked, her heart thumping simply because he was in the same house, almost directly under the spot where she now stood.

"I believe he is here for Mr. Childe, ma'am. But the young gentleman has only now begun to shave, so there will be some delay. I thought you should be informed."

"Thank you, Peters. Offer Lord Clayburn some refreshments while he waits and make sure the fire is built up."

When he was gone, she returned to the hearth and continued to brush her hair, trying to pretend that nothing had changed. She did *not* feel her skin tingling. He was the *last* man in the universe she wanted in her house. She profoundly wished him at Jericho.

Five minutes later, she rushed to the standing wardrobe and pulled out the first dress she found with no hooks or buttons in the back. All her niggling doubts about Clayburn's scheme to reform Arthur had suddenly become a tidal wave of mistrust. It was past time she confronted him and demanded that he explain what he was about.

That was her excuse, anyway.

Unwilling to question her motives further, she pried her unstockinged feet into a pair of sandals and raced downstairs.

When she stepped nervously into the Red Saloon, she thought at first that Peters must have misdirected her. Then she spied a tall, still figure slumped on a wing-backed chair near the fireplace. On the side table next to him, a full glass of wine sat untouched.

He was asleep, she realized, silently drawing closer. Long legs in tight biscuit-colored breeches stretched toward the flagstone hearth. One arm was curled in his lap, and the other dangled over the side of the chair. His head lay against the wing-back padding, a swatch of dark hair fallen over his brow. His mouth was slightly open.

She leaned against the wall near the fireplace and looked her fill of him.

Except for one brief nod, when they chanced to meet in the foyer before he led Arthur away, she had not seen Clayburn for more than a week. His skin was paler than before, she noted critically, and there were dark shadows under his eyes.

But he was beautiful still, even with those faint lines of dissipation near his temples and at the corners of his lips. His chest rose and fell with the steady rhythm of his breathing. In sleep, he seemed younger. Guileless, although she knew he was nothing of the sort.

The man was simply worn down by a weeklong marathon of debauchery. Suddenly infuriated at the waste of it all, she sprang forward and kicked him on the shin.

"Bloody hell!" He shot upright in the chair, rubbing his leg. "What the devil was *that* about?"

"Just trying to get your attention," she replied genially.

"Pretend I have stood and bowed and greeted you properly, you rag-mannered wench. Because I'm damned if I will." He smothered a yawn behind his hand. "If you mean to give me a rake-down, I assure you that I am in no mood to listen."

"Your moods, Lord Clayburn, do not concern me. I merely wish an accounting of Arthur's progress, or his decline, whichever applies. Until he bumbled in this morning, he had been gone more than forty hours in a row. Where have you been?"

Clayburn frowned, as if trying to remember. "An inn about thirty miles from here. I think. We went to a cockfight, and then to a mill. Or was it wrestling? Men fought, at any rate, and we wagered on the outcome. Later, a few young bucks commandeered a pair of mail coaches and set out to race them to High Wycombe. You will be glad to hear I plucked Arthur from the driver's bench before he took the reins. We rode inside. And won."

"Congratulations," she said. "How proud you must be."

"Not in the slightest. I meant him to come home with his pockets to let, but Arthur recouped a week of losses on that stupid race. Now I must see to it he loses every groat of it tonight at the hells." He yawned again. "Tell you what, Francesca. I am too old for this nonsense. If my plans for this evening fail, I wash my hands of the whole business. Enough is enough."

"Why not call it off now? What little faith I had that you would succeed is gone, and even you are ready to abandon hope."

"Not quite." He stood and shook his whole body like a wet dog. "When this is over, I plan to sleep for a month. Meantime, point me in Arthur's direction. We need to have a private talk before going out."

Francesca passed him to a footman and spent the next few minutes wrestling with her conscience.

Her conscience lost. Removing her sandals, she tiptoed upstairs and huddled against the wall next to

165

Arthur's room, ear pressed to the closed door. But she could hear nothing through the heavy oak and was about to turn away when a servant emerged, carrying a shaving basin.

A mad charade ensued, she trying to keep him quiet and waving wildly when he moved to close the door behind him, he gaping at her with an earnest effort to interpret her gyrations. At last, with a shrug, he left the door cracked open and went on his befuddled way.

With care, she positioned herself where she could see without being seen through the narrow slit, managing an excellent view of Arthur at his dressing table. Clayburn, invisible from all angles, was speaking.

". . . what you have been clamoring for."

"A brothel?" Arthur bounced with excitement. "That's famous, sir!"

Brothel? Oh, dear Lord!

"Sometimes essential," Clayburn said in a dry voice. "Especially after a week in company with foul-breathed, unwashed men."

"But there are women in the hells, too. Didn't you notice? Some of them have rooms upstairs. They told me so. Invited me there," he added, preening smugly.

"I'm not surprised. But they are not women you wish to consort with."

"No indeed," Arthur agreed hastily. After a moment, he swallowed, causing his prominent Adam's apple to bob up and down. "May I ask precisely why?"

"The whole point of this discussion," Clayburn said, "is for you to ask any question that comes to mind. I do not mean to stand in place of your father, who should have explained these matters long since, but I rather doubt he has been of much help."

"None at all. And besides, he probably can't remember what it's like. We are young, and he is old. I never want to be old."

Francesca heard Clayburn sigh.

"Truly? Well, I certainly do. Not right away, of course, but I anticipate a pleasurable dotage as pudding to my wild salad days."

"Not me!" Arthur buttoned his waistcoat. "I mean to live hard, burn bright, and flame out like a Congreve rocket."

"How very theatrical."

Francesca wanted to applaud. She wished she could see Clayburn's face, but she knew his expressions well enough by now to imagine them with some accuracy.

"One day," he said, "when you are wise enough to appreciate her, I shall introduce you to Eudora Swann. She is four-and-eighty, I believe, and has rollicked through each day of her long life with vigor, passion, and joy. I expect she'll do the same for many years to come. And when she dies, she will flame out more gloriously than any rocket. Or any foolish boy with more bottom than sense."

Arthur paled.

"Take no insult," Clayburn said kindly. "I myself have only just begun to realize that life must not be held cheaply."

"But you still drink and gamble, sir. You go to cockfights and mills."

"Not so often as I used to. Keeping you entertained has been rather a challenge, young man."

Arthur looked confused. "I had thought you but seven or eight years older than I. No more than that."

"Assuredly. But the constant infusion of spirits has begun to leave me with devilish headaches. That won't happen to you for some time, but there will come a day when you wake up wishing you'd never been born. The merest whisper will sound in your head like an artillery barrage."

"It never seems to bother Papa," Arthur said. "He still drinks prodigiously."

"Only because he cannot help himself. He gambles for the same reason. And if you are heir to his addictions as well as his name, you will eventually become what he is now." Clayburn clapped his hands together. "But never mind all that. You are down from Oxford to enjoy yourself, and I am of a mood to do the same. Tonight we shall teach the devil to dance."

Arthur looked a trifle less enthusiastic than before. "What does that mean, sir?"

"Why, a bit of everything this side of perversion. First off, a fine dinner accompanied by the best wines, followed by several hours of dice and cards. Then on to Madame Fifi's House of Delights."

Francesca stifled a groan.

"Which brings me back to where this conversation began," Clayburn added after a moment. "Women. If you tell me you pass a single waking hour . . . make that ten minutes . . . without imagining a naked woman under your heaving body, you will astonish me."

"I won't astonish you," Arthur confessed, his face the color of a ripe tomato.

"I'll not probe your sordid past," Clayburn assured him. "But on the chance my own experiences may be relevant, I will tell you what I have learned from them. You may be spared a few of my mistakes." He paused. "Or perhaps you never amuse yourself with the town strumpets."

Arthur made a strangled noise.

"I certainly did," Clayburn said in a reminiscent tone. "But luckily, I made a friend among the senior students. He knew where the more fastidious ladies were to be found and cautioned me to avoid the ones I had been eyeing surreptitiously. The ones who wait on street corners, ready to exchange a toss for a shilling or two."

Impossibly, Arthur's face graduated to a brighter red. "What if a fellow only *has* a shilling or two?"

"Why, he gives the ladies a polite, respectful smile and keeps walking. But of course, if you persist in wanting to die young, by all means spend your shillings on alleyway doxies. Only keep in mind that they are often afflicted with the sort of diseases that will cause you to shrivel up, not flame out."

"Oh."

As Francesca watched, Arthur went from scarlet to paper-white. Really, she ought to stomp in and drag her hapless young cousin from the clutches of this rakehell before any more bits of carnal knowledge were transferred.

But no parts of her body would move. All parts felt hot and quivery, some more than others. And each and every one stayed in place as she listened, more fascinated by Clayburn's revelations than Arthur could ever be.

"If you have money," Clayburn said, "you can afford to be more selective. Before setting out for an evening of pleasure, I make sure to have enough to buy the very best. Or I was used to, back when I found it necessary to pay for a bed partner."

Francesca went rigid.

"You don't pay?" Arthur asked incredulously. "I was told a man got married or he paid. Usually both."

"Not wholly inaccurate. But like most generalities, it excludes the more discerning options. For instance, some men wed happily and remain faithful to their wives. Others would like to, but until a love match is found, they must opt for celibacy. . . . I shudder at the thought . . . or the careful middle ground."

Which is? Francesca wondered.

"Which is?" Arthur asked.

"Ah, that's difficult to explain. But for the most part, it has to do with controlling oneself at all times, which is exceedingly troublesome. I know, because I have too often run amok when temptation overwhelmed me. We have run amok together for the last several nights. Great fun, eh?"

"Oh yes," Arthur responded fervently. Then he frowned. "You never explained about the women, sir. Why you can choose without paying. But I suppose it's because of how you look."

"To an extent," Clayburn agreed easily. "Widows and fashionable ladies of easy virtue flock to me, but I take no credit for that. My appearance is an accident of fate, and while it may attract the women, it cannot hold them beyond a quick infatuation. Nor should you rely on your own considerable physical attractions. May come a time when your hair thins, as has your father's. And if you spend all your time drinking and lazing about, you will soon grow a paunch. More important, if you fail to secure an education, the ladies will find you a tedious companion and cast you off."

Arthur raised his bony chin. "Is this meant to be a lecture, sir? I hear enough of those at chapel."

"And pay them no heed whatever, I collect." Clayburn laughed. "Nor did I. In fact, I took my degree at Oxford only because my father would have filleted me with a spoon if I failed to emerge with honors. Your father is not so demanding, to your great good fortune. Or perhaps he hopes you will abandon the university so that he'll not have to stand the fees."

"Oh, Sotherton does that. Sends pocket money, too."

Francesca swallowed a growl of protest. She had not been aware that Papa was subsidizing Arthur's education, although she ought to have guessed.

"You have been gaming with the duke's money? May I suggest you not mention this to Miss Childe? Or anything else she would be offended to hear?"

"I'm never so sap-skulled as to do that!" Arthur began to wrap a cravat around his neck. "A man of the world don't talk to females about matters of importance. Right, sir?"

Man of the world indeed! Francesca thought scornfully.

" 'The better part of valor is discretion,' " Clayburn agreed. "Finish dressing yourself, please, and waste no time experimenting with your neckcloth. You'll be removing it soon enough, or allowing a woman to perform the service for you."

While Francesca conjured up that repugnant image, a fatal few seconds went by. And by the time she realized that Clayburn was headed for the passageway, there was nothing for it but to draw herself up and pretend she had only just arrived.

He wasn't the least bit fooled. Without pausing, he seized her elbow as he strode past and led her relentlessly to the downstairs parlor.

"I was coming to see if you wished the carriage brought around," she said brightly.

"Humbug." His eyes flashed. "You were eavesdropping."

The tips of her ears ignited. "Very well, so I was. But I only learned such shambag behavior from you! Or have you forgot skulking among the bookshelves at Hatchard's to listen in on my—"

"You were talking about *books*, Francesca. And in

171

a public place, where any number of people might have overheard. This circumstance was altogether different, as you are well aware. Arthur and I were having a private, man-to-man conversation."

"More like rutting-beast-to-rutting-beast," she fired back. "It's a blessing I chanced to come by in time to put a stop to this. Fifi's House of Delights indeed! You will not take that innocent boy to a brothel, Clayburn. I forbid it!"

"As you wish," he said indifferently. "For myself, I'd greatly prefer a good night's sleep. But when you tell him of your decision, I strongly suggest you not use the term *boy*."

"I won't." Flustered, she wrung her skirt with both hands. "I mean, *you* are the one who must speak to him. Inform Arthur that you have changed your mind."

"Oh, no, my dear. You will play despot on your own. And endure the consequences, too, for I promise he will immediately set out to prove his manhood in ways you do not wish to know about. Think on it a moment. If he will not tolerate lectures or discipline from me, a man he is misguided enough to idolize, how will he react to coercion by a pestilential female?"

Sinking onto the nearest chair, she studied her fingernails intently. "Then what am I to do?"

He came to her, so close that his knees touched hers. "This row is my fault, I know, because I failed to discuss everything with you beforehand. But these are not matters a man can easily discuss with a woman, Francesca. I hoped you might simply trust me, just this once. Surely you cannot believe I have set myself to corrupt the boy?"

"I don't know what to believe," she said plaintively. "He is so young and so incredibly foolish. Even you call him a boy."

"Never to his face, I assure you. For the past week he has been my boon companion, bang up to the mark in every way. A fine fellow to broach a bottle with, although he has twice cast up his accounts on my boots. A clever gamester, despite the fact he has lost on every wager until that mail coach race. He is living the life he has always dreamed of, and it is slowly turning into a nightmare. But he will never admit that, don't you see? Male pride is a fearsome thing. Insult him now and he is lost forever."

She gazed up into a pair of remarkably sympathetic eyes. "But a *brothel*, Clayburn?"

"The coup de grâce," he said, lowering himself to one knee before her. "You should know that Arthur is not so innocent as you wish to think, nor so experienced as he likes to imagine. Unless Oxford has changed radically since I was there, he has experimented with a few of the town fillies. I would be greatly surprised if he'd failed to do the same during his last few years at Eton. He is nineteen, Francesca. Few males survive to that age in possession of their virginity."

She supposed he was right. But then, as a virgin of one-and-thirty, she knew precious little about the business. "I shall take your word for that," she said in a resigned voice. "But how can an evening with Madame Fifi's Barques of Frailty convince him to return to school? It's more likely to have the opposite effect, I would imagine."

"Ah, but this particular evening will not live up to his expectations," Clayburn said with a wry grin. "Nor will he. Must I go into detail?"

"Not *vivid* detail, I beg you. But give me some reason to approve this ramshackle strategy. At the moment, I am certain you and Arthur are a matched pair of swine."

His mouth tightened. "Suffice it to say that I have already made arrangements with the young woman who will entice Arthur to her bedchamber. By then he will be quite drunk, for I shall see to that at the gaming hells we mean to visit first. An excess of wine wreaks havoc with a man's ability to perform. And in the unlikely case his virility outpaces the wine and his current state of exhaustion, Miss Lily has been well paid to make sure he embarrasses himself."

"To what purpose?" she asked, wholly confused. And wildly curious, although she would never admit it.

"Never you mind," he said firmly. "He will boast to me of his prowess as we make our way home, and I shall pretend to believe him. Leave him alone tomorrow, Francesca. For God's sake, don't nag or question him. He has decisions to make, and they won't come easily. But I'll wager anything you like that he will give you, before suppertime, some face-saving excuse for returning to Oxford."

"And I, pretending to regret his departure, will provide funds to see him there. And a bit more, so that he can buy a few rounds while he regales his schoolfellows with the account of his adventures in company with London's most notorious rake. Have I got it right, my lord?"

"Something like that, yes," Clayburn said approvingly. "One more thing. Be generous when you open Sotherton's purse. If Arthur cuts a swash at Oxford, he'll be all the more eager to remain there. And with luck, he will heed some of the advice I was attempting to provide a few minutes ago. You heard most of it, but I doubt you understood the significance. 'Twas for his own good, I promise."

One swine telling another swine how to rut with a bit of discrimination, she thought crossly. How very charming. "I'm sure you meant well," she said.

Wincing, he came to his feet just as Arthur launched himself into the parlor.

"Hullo, Cesca. We're off now."

Francesca pinned a smile on her lips. "Enjoy your evening, gentlemen. And, Arthur, secure a house key from Peters before you leave. No telling what time you'll be home, and I don't wish to keep a servant posted at the door all night. By the way, that waistcoat suits you, and your neckcloth is a thing of wonder. How do you manage to dress so well without a valet?"

Arthur flushed with pleasure at the compliment. "Lord Clayburn is teaching me how to go on," he said with a bow to his mentor.

"Well done," Clayburn murmured in her ear as Arthur went off to find the butler. "Stay the course and he will soon be back where he belongs."

"He had better be," she warned. "Otherwise, I shall come at you with a poker and beat your brains out. Assuming you have any," she added waspishly.

"That's my girl." He ruffled her hair. "Obdurate to the last. Remind me, when this business with Arthur is done with, that I still have a gift for you. Perhaps two, although I begin to despair of the second."

Wasn't that just like a man? she thought as he bowed and went to join his protégé. He implied, but he never *said*. This was the second time he'd mentioned a gift, the first a whole week ago, but she'd yet to receive so much as a potted violet from him.

She ached to run after him and demand clarification. So what that Arthur was destined for failure with his light-skirt? Clayburn never spoke of how he planned to spend his own time at Madame Fifi's.

Which meant that she would probably spend *her* evening imagining him in bed with a doxy.

Chapter 15

Love's a boundless burning waste,
Where bliss's stream we seldom taste.
　　　　　　　　—*Thomas Campbell*

A cavalry regiment, mounted on elephants, stomped through Clay's restless dreams. The great beasts circled his bed, their huge hooves pounding. Pounding.

Clay rolled over and buried his head under the pillow, but the thumping persisted. A blacksmith must be beating his brains out on an anvil, he decided, not sorry for it. The sooner the job was done with, the better.

"Open the damn door, Clay!"

Jerry's shout hit him with the force of an explosion. He bolted upright, moaning as sunlight daggered through the slit in the curtains and stabbed his aching eyes.

"Go away," he moaned.

More thumping and shouting from the passageway. Damn! Lurching to his feet, he grabbed at the bedpost for support. Then, glancing down, he apprehended that he was naked, although he'd no recollection of removing his clothes. Or of arriving in his rooms, for that matter.

With a struggle, he contrived to stuff his legs into the breeches he'd discarded on the floor. Must have, he thought muddily, for there they lay.

"I know you're in there!" *Thump thump thump*.

Clay staggered across the room and wrestled with

the key as he vaguely plotted ways to murder his former friend. Stood to reason a *real* friend would shut the devil up and go away.

When the lock clicked, Jerry burst into the room, all but knocking Clay off his feet. "About time, you—" His mouth dropped. "My God! What in blue blazes happened last night? Madame Fifi beat the stuffing out of you?"

Clay shook his head, immediately regretting it. The slightest move ignited firecrackers where his brain used to reside. He stumbled to the bed and lowered himself gently at the edge. "She wanted me, I think. But I only meant to wait in the parlor for Arthur. She kept plying me with champagne. God, I'll never touch that devil's brew again as long as I live. Which won't be very much longer, if I'm lucky."

"So you've got a hangover," Jerry said unsympathetically. "Too bad. Now, pull yourself together, because we have a *real* problem. Livvy's scarpered with Heston. According to her note, they are on their way to Gretna."

"Good riddance to them both." Clay rubbed his forehead with a shaky hand. His mouth tasted of cotton and old fish, and a beachful of gritty sand had lodged under his eyelids. "Now they can torment each other instead of plaguing the rest of us."

"I care no more what becomes of them than you do. Or I would not, except that Ann is concerned for her sister. Twins are close, y'know, even when they are nothing alike."

"Then *you* go hunt them down. I've had it up to my eyebrows with that spawn of Satan. If the chit wants Heston, I say let her have him. A marriage made in hell."

Jerry poured water from a pitcher on the side table into a glass. "Drink this," he ordered. "And try

177

to pay attention. Francesca means to set out after them."

"*What?*" A mouthful of water spewed across the floor. "She can't be so muttonheaded as that."

"Well, I'm not certain she intends to chase them all the way up the Great North Road. Hard to tell. She's in a fearsome temper right now."

"I can imagine." Clay sat straighter, trying to focus his eyes. "You had better fill me in."

"Finally!" Jerry found a pair of boots under a chair and launched them onto the bed. "Get dressed. When I arrived at the house an hour ago, meaning to pay a call on Ann, everyone was in a turmoil. Francesca had all the servants lined up for questioning, but apparently none of them saw Livvy go out."

"Give me times," Clay said, pulling on a boot. "We need to figure how much of a head start she's got."

"That's what Francesca was working on. They all returned from the ball about three o'clock, and Livvy told her maid not to disturb her until she rang. Said she meant to sleep well past noon. Arthur was the one found her room empty, about ten o'clock. He went in to say good-bye."

Thank God for that much, Clay thought. Arthur had seen the light. "Tell me he's on the way back to Oxford."

"He is. Mind you, he wanted to stay for all the excitement, but Francesca sent him packing. He looked almost as bad as you do, I must say."

"Thank you." Clay reeled to his dressing table and gazed at his reflection in the shaving mirror. Two red-rimmed, bloodshot eyes stared back. His hair stood out from his scalp like wagon spokes, and through the dark stubble of his beard, his skin was white as flour paste. "I see what you mean," he said with a groan.

"Go downstairs and order some hot water, will you? I need a shave."

"No time for that." Jerry picked up a shirt from the floor, sniffed at it, and threw it back in disgust. "Before I got there, Francesca had already dispatched footmen to find out where Heston has his rooms. Soon as she has the address, she'll go after him." He went to the stand of drawers and located a fresh shirt. Tossing it to Clay, he rummaged for a cravat. "Naturally I lied when she asked if I knew his direction. Said I would find out and came here."

Clay yanked on the shirt. "Good thinking. But if Heston plans a Scottish wedding, they'll be well on their way by now."

"Francesca thinks he don't mean to marry Livvy at all. She may be right. Heston's a blackguard, but he's no fool. Can you imagine being shackled to that goosecap for the rest of your life?" Jerry shuddered. "Anyway, she suspects this may be a plot to blackmail the Duke of Sotherton. He's in bad health, you know. Francesca is worried about the shock to his heart and will do anything to stop them. She also thinks they may still be in London or holed up somewhere close by."

For a moment Clay was tempted to let Francesca find Heston on her own. The man didn't stand a chance against that Italian virago. First she would scratch his eyes out. Then she'd do him *serious* harm.

Clay abandoned his efforts to tie a passable cravat and knotted the starched muslin loosely around his throat. "Did you come by hack or horse?" he asked as Jerry passed him a riding coat from the armoire.

"Nag. An urchin is holding him in the street."

"Good. Run down to the mews and bring Galahad around. With luck, we'll beat Francesca to Heston's flat. It's no more than a mile from here."

When Jerry was gone, Clay finished dressing, swiped a brush through his hair, and headed downstairs. On second thought, he went back to his rooms and located his sword stick. He'd itched to fight Heston for nearly two decades, and if anyone was to be transported for slitting his throat, it would not be Francesca Childe.

The journey to Heston's flat was accomplished within a few minutes, but they were already too late. Clay swore fervently when he recognized Francesca's carriage drawn up in front of the tall town house. Somehow, she had unearthed the address and arrived in record time.

"Not altogether bad," Jerry pointed out as they handed the reins to a pair of eager street boys. "She'd be on her way again if Heston weren't to home."

A surly landlord directed them to the second floor, wholly unnecessary since Francesca's voice could be heard by anyone in the building. Clay and Jerry followed the sound of her tirade and peered through a crack in the door. It was partly open and led to a small parlor.

Heston, one arm stretched on the mantelpiece and legs crossed in a languid posture, looked singularly bored. Ann and Livvy were seated together on a small divan, holding hands.

And in the center of the room, practically glowing with fury, Francesca raged at Heston, and then at Livvy, and back at Heston again.

For a time, Clay held Jerry in the passageway. His goddess was on a rampage. And glory be, it was not directed at him.

Unfortunately, Heston's sharp eyes caught them out. "Ah, do come in, gentlemen. So long as we are to have a circus here, clowns are more than welcome."

Jerry immediately rushed to Ann and stood behind

her with his hands on her shoulders. Clay stepped inside, taking time to close the door, and leaned against it with his arms folded.

Silenced for the moment, Francesca was staring at him as if he'd just emerged from a peat bog.

"You look like hell, Clayburn," Heston observed amiably. "Horse sit on your face?"

Francesca found her tongue again. "This is *not* a joking matter, Lord Heston. And you have yet to explain yourself."

"Only because you've not given me the opportunity to speak, Miss Childe. Since opening the door to you, which I've frankly come to regret, you have held the floor. And I had thought Livvy impossible to silence."

Clay saw Francesca's black eyes go even hotter and decided to intervene before she went for blood. "I suggest you talk to *me*, Heston. Exactly what is going on here?"

"Damned if I know. Perhaps you can sort it out, although to look at you, I'm inclined to doubt it. For that matter, how is this any of your business?"

"I choose to make it my business," Clay replied evenly.

"Oh, well, then. I must, perforce, confess all." He shot a glance at Livvy. "This bumblebroth was stirred up last evening when, much to my surprise, Miss Olivia Childe proposed marriage to me."

When Francesca erupted with a rush of Italian, Clay lifted a hand and shook his head. To his surprise, she clamped her lips together. Good girl, he thought, turning back to Heston. "Can you have mistaken the young lady's intentions?"

"Hardly. Livvy has no acquaintance with subtlety, as you must surely know. Naturally I was flattered and honored by her offer, and what is more, I accepted. But

181

I rather expected our nuptials would take place sometime in the distant future, when she had grown up and
learned to conduct herself like a real lady instead of
the rag-mannered brat she is."

He favored the brat with a cordial smile. "I'm not
at all averse to wedding her, you understand. We
share a mutual distaste for rules of any sort and
cannot tolerate a bit in our mouths. In very many
ways, we are well suited to each other."

"But neither of you has a feather to fly with,"
Francesca objected. "How are you to live?"

"On our wits?"

When Francesca glowered, his eyes hardened. "You
needn't fear we'll cling to your purse strings, Miss
Childe. Livvy has explained that you stand to inherit
Sotherton's fortune, and what little Bromley receives
along with the title will not outlast his forays at the
gaming tables."

Flushing hotly, Francesca cast a swift look at Clay.
She was gauging his reaction to the news, he col-
lected. He struggled to maintain a passive expression
on his face, as if the information were of no import to
him. But his heart was turning great somersaults in
his chest.

Oh, damn. Why must she be wealthy? He felt the
ground cut out from under him. Anything that pre-
served her independence subtracted from his hopes.
Now he understood that she had absolutely no reason
to accept anything but a love match. And from all he
could tell, she was a far sight from loving *him*.

"Why must you all interfere?" Livvy demanded
shrilly. Bounding up, she rushed to Heston's side and
seized his arm. "Except for Ann, not a one of you
gives a fig what becomes of me. Father cares nothing
for any of his children, even Arthur, because we are a
nuisance to him. Cesca, you only wish me to stop

making trouble long enough to find a husband, so that you can be rid of me, too. Well, just see, I have found a husband."

"Ah, but you continue making trouble," Heston pointed out.

"It's the only way I can ever get what I want," she retorted. "And if you'd spent even a week in Rutlandshire, not the lifetime I endured there, you would be a bit of a monster, too."

"I daresay." He smiled down at her. "But Miss Childe has your best interests at heart, you know."

"Yes, I'm sure of it. But her heart is vastly different than mine, Rupert. The only thing she truly wants is to go home." Livvy cast pleading eyes in Francesca's direction. "Don't you see? You can wash your hands of me now. And when Jerry rouses himself to make an offer, which I'm certain he means to do, Ann will surely accept. Isn't it famous? We are both fired off. You need not give the ball you've been dreading or shepherd us to any more tedious affairs. You ought to be pleased, Cesca. And happy for us!"

Unfair, you nasty little witch, Clay thought in the agonizing silence that followed. Ann's cheeks flamed with humiliation, and Jerry looked as if he were about to sink through the floorboards. Heston remained sardonically aloof, but the tight hand clamped on Livvy's shoulder was a clear reproach.

Alone in the center of the room, Francesca stood tall and splendidly regal, but her lips trembled with uncertainty. He could not mistake the hurt in her eyes. After all she had done and endured for Livvy, to be dismissed in such a fashion!

Clay knew better than to go to her now, although he ached to console her. But he could best help by drawing attention to himself until she recovered her composure, although later, he supposed, she would comb him down for meddling.

"An interesting summary of events," he said with a nod to Livvy. "But you neglected to include the scandal that will attach to Ann and all your family if you make a bolt for the border."

"To which I have not agreed," Heston observed mildly.

"A rare venture into the realm of good sense," Clay acknowledged. "But neither did you return Livvy to her family immediately after she appeared at your door. Quick action on your part would have spared everyone this scene."

"True enough. But, my dear Clayburn, have you not realized that Livvy is impossible to budge once she has set her mind on a thing? I might have hauled her kicking and screaming through the streets to Grosvenor Square, of course. But I chose to await reinforcements, and lo, you have come to my rescue. Among us, five against one, we may be able to subdue her."

"Infamous!" Livvy broke from Heston's grip and turned on him. "I have risked everything for you. Even the affection of my sister, and I do love Ann, although I use her badly. You will *not* send me back, Rupert. I won't have it!"

Heston's smile was uncommonly sweet. "But what choice have we, my love? Alienating what few friends and relations we can claim, odious creatures that we are, is a poor way to begin a life together. I'll not take you to Gretna."

Sobbing, she threw herself at his chest. And after a moment, rolling his eyes, he opened his arms and drew her into an embrace.

Clay was unsure what to make of this. He glanced at Francesca, who seemed equally confused. "Shall we come to the point?" he asked, jabbing a finger in Heston's direction. "Do you mean to wed her?"

"Oh, eventually. When she is of age. Perhaps on her birthday, if she conducts herself properly in the meantime."

"B-but that's eight m-months from now," Livvy wailed. "I cannot wait so long. Abominable man. If you really loved me, you would carry me off this very instant."

Francesca pressed her hands together. "Consider, Livvy. Only a man whose affections are casually engaged would demand immediate gratification. The man who is truly in love stays the course, however long and rocky it may be."

Livvy glanced over her shoulder, arrested by a revelation that had clearly never occurred to her. Then she frowned. "Perhaps so, for others. But in this case, I think it's better to seal the bond right away. Rupert is handsome, charming, and poor. A woman with a fortune is like to steal him from me. And then I'd murder her, which would be a greater scandal than elopement."

Sometimes, Clay reflected, even a widgeon made good sense. But Francesca had gone white.

"Do you want the sort of husband who could be won over by money?" she asked. "Or a miserable piece of land? Lord Heston has declared himself willing to accept an impoverished bride. He has, for your own good, promised to wait until you are of age. Is it not time you repay him with a sacrifice of your own?"

Livvy lifted a hand to Heston's cheek. "I suppose. But all I have to give is my whole self, and that is pitifully little. I am a horrid girl, just as everybody tells me. You think I don't know it, but I do. And I'm not likely to change very much. That scares me, Rupert."

"It frightens me, too," he said softly. "But we shall deal well enough together."

Jerry cleared his throat. "Not to interfere, but has anybody considered that they can marry right away? We only need Lord Bromley to give his consent."

Everyone looked to Heston for a response. Or that was Clay's impression, since he still suspected Heston meant to use any excuse to avoid wedding Livvy. Not once in all the years Clay had known the man had he exhibited the slightest trace of honor. This display of concerned affection for Livvy and her family could only be a sham.

Livvy plucked at his shoulders with both hands. "Rupert?"

Heston shrugged. "If Bromley steps forward with his approval, I'll purchase a special license and we can do the deed immediately. But I have not seen him about this last week or more. Anyone know where he can be found?"

Attention swung to Clay.

"What?" He held out his arms. *"I* haven't seen him either. Not since Wolvercote."

"But you could find him," Francesca said. Her enormous brown-black eyes blazed with hope. "You did so before. Will you at least try, my lord?"

Oh *hell*! Another shamble through the gin mills, flash houses, and back alleys of London in pursuit of Bromley Childe. Bloody, miserable, *hell hell hell!*

He bowed politely. "As you wish, Miss Childe."

Chapter 16

Good-bye, knight, go your way,
I hear my father calling me.
                                    —*Provençal Song*

After scouring every gaming hell, gin mill, cockpit, and lowlife establishment in London, Clay finally thought to hire a Bow Street Runner.

Second only to fixing his attentions on Francesca, it was the best idea he'd ever had. Mr. Worbel quickly learned that Bromley had taken a public coach in the direction of Brighton, and they set off together to look for him there.

When that lead flamed out, they worked their way back toward London, inquiring at every posthouse where the London-to-Brighton coaches changed horses. Every day Clay considered returning to London, leaving Mr. Worbel to complete the search on his own, but he could not bear to let Francesca down. So he plodded on, inn by inn, town by town, for more than a week.

Finally, thanks to a postboy with a good memory, Bromley was traced to, of all places, Tunbridge Wells.

A favorite watering place for dowagers, refined widows, and gentlemen not in the first blush of youth, it was the most unlikely spot for Bromley to land. But there he was, starkly sober and with a slightly bewildered expression engraved on his face, firmly in the clutches of one Mrs. Phemia Vertue.

The widow of a well-to-do tradesman, Mrs. Vertue

was happily parading his lordship at the local assemblies to impress her friends and, most especially, her enemies. Short but solidly built, with a voice like thunder, she put Clay forcibly in mind of a battering ram.

Bromley had no objection to ridding himself of the twins. Quite the contrary. But since a thug to whom he owed money had promised to break his knees unless he paid up, he meant to keep well away from London for the next fifty years. It seemed that Clay would have to settle for carrying back his written consent to the marriages.

But when Mrs. Vertue heard the tale, she immediately offered to cover her dear Bromley's debt and rig him out in fine style for the ceremony. For the chance to rub shoulders with the nobs at a Society wedding, she would probably have dragged him to London by his hair.

And now, at long last, Clay was on his way to pay court to his goddess, the Petrarch burning a hole in his coat pocket. He chuckled, wondering what Francesca was making of her surprise houseguest. The widow's coach-and-four must have arrived at Grosvenor Square late yesterday afternoon, followed by another carriage loaded with trunks and portmanteaus.

Of a certain, Francesca would be pleased with *him*. For the first time since meeting her, he felt very sure of himself. Everything she had asked of him, he had done. And when he wasn't chasing down Bromley and Livvy, or setting Arthur on the straight and narrow, he'd spent every waking moment working on his poem.

Yes indeed, he'd been a veritable saint, martyr, knight, and poet, all rolled into one. The goddess could find no fault with him now.

When he arrived at her town house, the butler greeted him with more than his usual disdain, waving him churlishly into a foyer stacked with trunks and boxes and leaving him there while he ascertained if Miss Childe was receiving company.

Puzzled, Clay watched two footmen carry another large trunk down the stairs and deposit it in the foyer with a groan of relief. He was about to ask them what was going on when the butler reappeared, beckoning him along the narrow passageway instead of leading him upstairs to one of the parlors. More confused than ever, he trailed a few paces behind to a door near the rear of the house.

"Miss Childe is in the library," the butler said curtly, his hand on the latch. "She instructed me to ask if you wish any refreshment."

"That will not be necessary," Clay replied, wondering what he had done in recent memory to set the man's back up. Or perhaps Peters's surly mood had something to do with all those boxes in the foyer.

Reminding himself that he, at least, was in a very good mood indeed, Clay stepped through the door Peters grudgingly opened, looking around for Francesca.

"My lord," she said with a formal curtsy.

He bowed in return, automatically, a sensation of dread creeping up his spine.

She stood behind a large oak desk, which was cluttered with papers from corner to corner. She wore a plain, dark green dress. Her hair, barely contained in a loose braid, reached nearly to her waist.

She gazed at him politely, as if greeting a stranger. "Do forgive the racket and disorder, Lord Clayburn. Except for the public rooms, we are preparing the house to be closed down."

"But why?" He felt as if he'd wandered onto the moon. "Surely you mean to stay in London for the Season?"

"No indeed, sir, I return to Rutlandshire the very day after the wedding. Weddings, to be precise."

"I see," he said, although he didn't see at all. Oh dear God. *How soon?* was his first thought. He had not meant to declare himself this very afternoon. On the contrary. He'd intended to arrange a romantic proposal, on a sunny afternoon by the River Thames, with flowers and champagne and perhaps a violinist. He would read his poem to her, and drop to one knee before her, and tell her what was in his heart.

But like every other fantasy in which he'd indulged since meeting his goddess, this one, the one he'd most longed to create for both of them, had suddenly become impossible. And he had no idea why.

Through stinging eyes, he saw Francesca sink onto her chair and gesture to him to seat himself across the desk from her. Instead, he began to pace the room, struggling to order his wits. "Has a wedding d-date been fixed?"

"Not quite yet. Lord Heston and Jerry secured special licenses a few days ago. Now they are scouring the parishes for a church and vicar. Only one church, thank heavens, since we are to have a single ceremony. With luck, they'll find a location for Saturday next."

"But that is only three days away!"

"Yes, well, you may recall that Livvy is a trifle impatient. She wants to get on about it, and quite honestly, so do the rest of us."

He stopped himself before tripping over a footstool. "You are aware, I presume, that everyone will suspect other reasons for the hurried marriages."

"They may think what they like," she replied calmly. "In any case, we will invite a great many prominent guests to our *hurried* wedding breakfast, where they may quiz the brides and grooms and judge for themselves. At the least, my lord, we will serve up two love matches in a single morning, which is wonder enough in this cynical town. And we will all be long gone before the gossips begin to dissect the whats and whys of it."

Well said, he approved silently, still unable to link his tongue to his brain. *Francesca is leaving!* And from everything he could tell so far, without a single thought for him.

She made a sweeping gesture over the desk. "As you can see, Lord Clayburn, I am busily compiling a list of guests, and will begin writing a hundred invitations or more when the wedding date is firmly fixed. Maria Beaton, bless her, is arranging flowers and catering, but even so, I have much to do this afternoon. Pray forgive me if I seem a bit distracted."

He cleared his throat. "Shall I assume, under the circumstances, that Bromley arrived with the paternal go-ahead?"

"Oh, yes." A smile curved her lips and quickly vanished. "Widow in tow. Rather the other way around, actually. A most fettlesome woman, don't you think?"

"There was no stopping her from accompanying Bromley," he said ruefully. "I did try."

"No matter. She will keep him on good behavior through the wedding and breakfast, which is my only concern. After that, he may go to Hades with my blessing. Although I rather suspect Mrs. Vertue has plans of her own for Bromley. But however it shakes out, Lord Clayburn, you may be sure that I will never again send you off to find my dear uncle."

"I am relieved to hear it." He propped his shoulders against a bare bookshelf and folded his arms. "Naturally I take great pleasure in performing services for you, Miss Childe, and will do so again at the next opportunity. But one does relish a bit of variety."

That was supposed to make her smile. Instead, he saw her mouth tighten. Her gaze darted from the desk to the windows to the door. Everywhere but to him. A hard lump settled in his chest. What the bloody hell had gone wrong in the last ten days?

For all practical purposes, he had been the very model of a virtuous gentleman since meeting her. Every venture into the places where he had once run wild— the gaming hells, Wolvercote, even that one innocent night at a brothel—had been taken on her behalf.

Now, her twin charges about to marry and all her goals achieved, she had gone cold on him. Francesca in a temper, he could deal with. He longed for her to rage at him, because there was always truth in her fury. But the vast distance between them was unspoken, and the barriers she had erected invisible. He could not think how to reach her.

It occurred to him this awful silence could have a simple explanation after all. He had devoted ten days and nights to tracking Bromley, and she could not have anticipated the difficulty of the task. Now she felt guilty. That must be it.

"If you are working yourself up to a speech of gratitude," he said, "please spare us both. It has been my greatest pleasure to be of assistance."

"I know. That is, I understand. It makes everything so much easier for you. And so much more difficult for me. I cannot think how to begin." She twisted the inkwell stopper around and around. " 'Thank you' is woefully inadequate in one way and ridiculous in the other, although I am certainly grateful. Without your help, Ann and Livvy would not be looking forward to the happiest day of their lives."

So why wouldn't Francesca look at him? He needed to see her eyes, because what she said made no sense whatsoever. What was it she *understood*? Why was a plain "thank you" *ridiculous*, of all things?

She picked up a pen and began stripping feathers from the quill. "It is long past time, of course, to clear the air between us. I take full responsibility. But in the beginning you were all but impossible to get rid of. And after that . . . well, never mind. Suffice it to say that your web was splendidly woven."

Tongue firmly lodged behind his clenched teeth, he made a vague gesture. By now, feathers were strewn over the blotter in front of her. And when she spoke, her face still turned down, her breath lifted them. They swirled around the way his mind was swirling, directionless.

He resumed his pacing. "Miss Childe," he said from near the window, "obviously you are distressed. But for the life of me, I cannot make out what it is you are trying to say."

Her head shot up. "Only that we should get this over with here and now, Lord Clayburn. It is best all around, don't you think?"

"I might, if I'd any idea what you were talking about." His heart began to jump crazily in his chest. "Have I offended in some way?"

"Oh, to be sure. But I do not take it at all personally. You have only done what you were told, after all. Short of the final step, of course, the one that requires you to come out from Montford's shadow and ask me to marry you. Face-to-face," she added, plucking madly at the few remaining feathers on her pen.

How else but face-to-face? Did she expect him to have a footman deliver his proposal? Wholly confused, he grabbed at the only thing she'd said that he understood. "What the devil has my father to do with this?"

"Oh, *please*! If not for him, you would never have paid me the slightest attention. Can you deny it?"

His mouth opened to do exactly that, then closed again as he recalled how his instant desire for her had become entangled with his stupid plan to marry the first woman he clapped eyes on.

"No, I cannot," he admitted. "Not altogether. There is no question I was captivated from the moment I saw you, but it took me a while to sort things out. I was still enraged after a bitter quarrel with the earl and caught up in a damned fool notion of marrying to spite him. Suddenly, there you were."

She was regarding him as if he'd turned green. "Captivated? Pah! Not by me, sir. You were *his* prisoner from the start. And how could marrying *me* serve any purpose but his own? Will you not have the decency to be honest, just this once?"

He was sure as hell trying. But however did she guess that the Earl of Montford came into this? Except for a niggling remnant of guilt, he'd all but forgotten his mad impulse to flaunt her before Montford's stunned eyes. Jerry might have let something slip, he supposed. Jerry was in love, and a besotted man said a great many things he never meant to own up to. As Clay was learning all too well.

"Look. I never imagined you would hear of this before I explained. Which I always meant to do," he hastened to add. "Well, after we were married, most like, but I would have told you eventually. Indeed, I rather thought you would find it amusing."

"Oh yes. Even now, I can scarce contain my laughter."

He released a harsh breath. "Is it so bad, Francesca? So I wanted you from the first. What man would not? And while I determined to have you for every wrong reason there can be, all those reasons vanished before

194

the sun came up again. So how are they of consequence? Even before I learned your full name and discovered that you were not a chaperone, I—"

"You thought I was a *chaperone*?" She banged a clenched hand on the desk, sending papers to the floor like confetti. "What nonsense. Even Bromley could devise a more convincing bouncer than that. Oh, I don't doubt for a moment you were astonished to encounter me at the inn, and I'm sure you didn't recognize me at first. How could you, since we had never met? But once you heard my name, you knew exactly who I was. And that you were supposed to marry me."

It finally began to dawn on Clay that they were speaking at cross-purposes altogether. She might as well have been addressing another man. He lunged for the one thing she'd said that truly mattered to him. For whatever reason, Francesca had expected him to propose marriage, and God knew he'd always meant to do so.

He drew himself up. "I had certainly hoped for a more fortuitous moment to say the words, but yes, I very much want you to be my wife. With all my heart."

"But of course," she said. "That was always clear, except that hearts have no place in a matter of business. Ironic, isn't it, that Montford went wrong from the start? Had he left the whole matter to you, he might well have succeeded."

Suddenly, Clay remembered his father's unexpected presence in London. The return of the commission money. The almost approving way Montford had spoken to him. Was it because he'd known that his son was courting Sotherton's daughter? Why the devil would he be glad of that?

Light dawned. Montford had somehow dug his talons into Francesca. He'd convinced her to turn his son away. What else could explain this nightmare? "Tell me," he said softly. "What has he done to you?"

"Oh, excellent!" She clapped her hands. "Were I not buried under with plans for a wedding, I'd draw this out if only to hear which clanker you'd next invent. But let us come to the point. I have read the letters, Lord Clayburn. One arrived every year, always in October, whereupon Papa and I had a good laugh. How could the earl, or you, imagine I'd be *grateful* for a husband willing to have me despite my mixed blood and illegitimate birth? Arrogant snobs! Montford would have done better to dispatch you with orders to seduce me. Sad to say, I'd probably have yielded without a struggle."

Letters? Oh God. Not this! He plastered one hand over his eyes. "Never tell me you are the bloody *Albatross*!"

"I beg your pardon?"

"I . . . no." He felt himself melting into his boots. "I never said that. It's just . . . I had no idea that you . . . Oh hell!"

"Truly, you belong on the stage, Lord Clayburn. Might I suggest you always play the Fool? You do it so well."

He felt like the Great King of All Fools. He hated his father more than he'd ever hated him before. He saw his dreams slipping away and the empty void that lay ahead, and he couldn't think how to snatch them back again.

Francesca was the wife his father had chosen for him? His precious, glorious, fiercest of goddesses was the Albatross? And worst of all, she'd known it all along? Well, she'd just said so, hadn't she?

Anger wrapped him up, winding around him until he could scarcely breathe. She had *known*! And played him along, probably laughing the way she'd done when Montford's letters arrived. What a joke, on every count. When she required a lackey to do her bidding, call on Clayburn. By his father's command, he would do whatever she asked of him. Act nursemaid to Livvy. Chase after Bromley from here to kingdom come. A wonder she hadn't demanded he clean the chimneys.

Such a fool he'd been, and she had played him for one. He crossed to the desk in three long strides. She looked back at him, clutching the pen in one hand and her skirt in the other. He realized she wasn't laughing at him at all. But her body was taut as a bowstring, and her chin was raised in that defiant way she had of taking on the world.

There had to be a way to stop this. Save them both. Damn it all, he *loved* her.

Hated her at the same time, for deceiving him, but that would pass. He resented her, too, for being the woman he didn't want, but already he knew that it no longer mattered. She couldn't help being the Albatross, any more than he could have stopped Montford from turning her against him before they ever met. But where to go from here?

"I knew that my father was determined to arrange a marriage of convenience," he said, choosing his words carefully. "Montford did everything in his considerable power to bend me to his will in this matter, and I was equally hell-bent to defy him. You may be sure that the woman he chose for me was the last woman on earth I would agree to wed."

"The Albatross."

"Just so. But I had no idea who she was. *Is*," he corrected swiftly.

"Oh, certainly not. Over a period of five years or more, your father attempted to negotiate a marriage, and in all that time he never told you the name of your future wife. Perfectly understandable."

"He may have done so. I cannot recall." Sweat broke out on his forehead. "That is to say, I formed an impression of her. You. *Not* you, clearly, but what I surmised from what he said."

"And what was that?" she asked too sweetly. "What impression of her, meaning me, did you derive?"

"Lord, I can hardly remember. Older than I am by several years, dowry that included land my father wanted. But what does any of that signify? Keep in mind that the earl and I keep well apart, by mutual choice, and I have schooled myself to listen to nothing he says. Your name, if it was told me, never registered."

"I see. Then I am to believe you encountered me by chance that night and fell instantly in love with a wet, bedraggled creature who snubbed you one minute and railed at you the next."

"At least you remember," he put in, like a drowning man clawing at the water. "That must count for something."

"Make nothing of it, sir. I lived three years on the streets of Naples and another eight-and-twenty in Rutlandshire. Any handsome aristocrat, however disreputable, would have caught my attention. Had we not met again, I'd easily have forgotten you."

"You were never to have the chance. I spent the next two weeks looking for you. I meant to find you again, Francesca."

"And you knew I'd be at Hatchard's that very afternoon, that very hour? An amazing feat. You do impress me, Lord Clayburn. You always have. A well-crafted marionette can be appreciated even by one who sees the Earl of Montford pulling your strings."

"Francesca." He was pleading now. "Listen to me. I didn't know."

Abruptly she stood and crossed swiftly to the door. "Likely we'll not meet again, Lord Clayburn, unless you mean to come to the wedding. Jerry will expect you, I suppose. In any case, I have much to do this afternoon, so please excuse me. You can let yourself out."

And then she was gone, while he stayed rooted in place like a tree stump. It took several minutes before he could move again, although he wasn't sure where to go. Well, out of the house. She'd dismissed him in no uncertain terms. If he'd possessed a tail, she'd have put a tinder-stick to it.

He still could not believe that it was truly over. There must be *some* way to make her understand.

But what if he managed to convince her that he'd fallen in love when he had no idea of her identity? It didn't necessarily follow that she would love him in return. From the beginning, she'd made it clear that he was everything she abhorred.

Never once had she wanted to spend time with him, talk with him, come to know him. No, she'd only called on the talents of a rakehell to accomplish what a decent man could not.

Despair settled over him. There had never been any hope. He had lost her even before he had begun.

At least he would have the satisfaction of thumbing his nose at Montford, he thought. Cold comfort indeed. On the whole, he'd rather be coshed on the head with a maco.

On numb feet, he made his way to the door. And then he remembered.

The book he'd nearly killed himself trying to find. She might as well have the damned thing. He pulled it from his pocket and tossed it on top of her desk.

Here are the words of a real poet, Francesca. You would not have liked my own poem nearly so well.

Chapter 17

Once, I dreamed of light. And then you came
on wings of fire, to set my soul aflame.
                    —*Galen Pender, Lord Clayburn*

From a tall box pew in St. George's, Hanover Square, Francesca watched Bromley Childe lead his daughters to the altar and give them over to their waiting bridegrooms.

Maria Beaton stood beside her, two handkerchiefs in her hand, after confessing that she always cried at weddings and rarely at funerals. That sounded reasonable enough to Francesca, for whom this day was a bit of both.

Livvy had babbled all the way down the aisle and found more to say at the altar. Finally the exasperated rector advised her to hush so that he could get on with business.

For once, Lord Heston had abandoned his usual sardonic pose. He gazed tenderly at his bride when she promised to love, honor, and obey, choking slightly on the last word. Ann wept with joy as she spoke her vows, and Jerry made her laugh when he stumbled over his own name.

Tears and laughter.

Francesca felt nothing at all.

She wanted to be happy, and knew she ought to be. Everything she'd come to London to do, she had accomplished. Or rather, Clayburn had accomplished for her. And certainly the brides and grooms had found happiness on their own, with no help from anyone.

All in all, she'd been pretty much useless. And she wanted to cry.

She had thought she would, bitterly and endlessly, after sending Clayburn on his way. But her eyes remained as arid as her heart. And really, she dared not let the pain come over her just yet. Perhaps she could weep tomorrow, alone in the carriage that would take her home. And try to think what to tell Papa of her adventures in London. Dear God, she would have to lie to him, too.

But she'd gotten very good at lying. And what could be more shameful than the lies she kept telling herself, after all? One day she might even convince herself that she was not in love with Clayburn.

Meantime, there was today to be endured. Only a few friends had been invited to the church, but more than a hundred guests were expected at the wedding breakfast to follow. This would be her sole opportunity to host the Fashionables who had welcomed her to their homes, and she meant to depart London on a note of triumph in that regard at least. Even the persnickety Lady Drummond-Burrell would find no fault with her lavish menu or the elegant decorations.

She had steeled herself for the ceremony, and she would make it through. She would *not* imagine standing at the altar with Clayburn while he took her hand to slip on the ring and made promises he could never keep. However much she wanted him, she had chosen not to settle for what little he would give her in return.

Thankfully, he'd not come to the wedding. Jerry, who had asked him to stand as groomsman because his brother had got the measles, was hurt when he declined with some vague excuse about a trip to

Brighton. To spare Jerry's feelings, she'd insisted that Prinny had long since commanded Clayburn's presence that particular weekend, although for all she knew, Prinny was firmly ensconced in London at this very moment.

But it was only one more lie, after all. She had told a lifetime's worth since meeting Clayburn.

Drat it! She *must* stop thinking about the man. Tomorrow I'll be gone, she reminded herself. Surely I can keep from falling to pieces for one more day.

While she was lost in her own thoughts, the wedding ceremony must have concluded. Lord Heston, with Livvy romping at his side, swept past the pew, followed more sedately by Jerry and Ann.

As she turned to watch them, Francesca saw a tall figure standing alone in the shadows at the back of the church. Her heart leaped to her throat.

"Can that be Clayburn?" Maria asked. "Isn't he supposed to be in Brighton?"

Francesca adjusted her cloak with numb fingers. "His plans must have changed at the last minute."

A pair of sharp brown eyes probed at her. Then Maria opened the pew door. "Very likely. Shall we join the others, my dear?"

Bromley, with the encroaching widow latched to his arm, intercepted them midway down the aisle. "Fine day, what? Popped 'em both off in one fell swoop. Hard to believe m'little girls are married ladies now."

Francesca couldn't help but smile. Bromley was positively beaming with pride, as if he had engineered this coup single-handedly. "I expect you'll soon have a grandchild or two to dandle on your knee," she said.

"Can't be a grandfather," he replied indignantly. "Too young."

Mrs. Vertue regarded him with fond forbearance. "Now, don't be tiresome, lovey. You're an old sot, but there's hope for you yet. And I'll be glad of grandbabies to coddle, so never you mind if those young bucks plant a seed or two this very night." She gave him a gap-toothed grin. "Not that you couldn't teach them a trick or two. There's lots to be said for experience."

With that, she bustled him off.

Maria broke out laughing. "My heavens, what an astonishing creature. 'Tis a wonder she didn't order the rector to preside over a third marriage while he was about it."

"She means to have him," Francesca agreed as they made their way to the vestibule. "But I cannot imagine why."

"I suspect she was planning to acquire a pet poodle when she met Bromley and set herself to housebreak a rackety aristocrat instead. He is all but nibbling out of her hand already."

"Which means she is like to become the next Duchess of Sotherton." Francesca shook her head. "Papa will think it all a great jest, of course."

Maria drew her to a halt. "You still mean to leave for home tomorrow, my dear? Is that a good idea?"

"Oh yes. Everything is arranged. I miss him, Maria, and he needs me. Except for the pleasure of your company, there is nothing to keep me in London now." She produced a quivery smile. "Well, except for that elusive dinner party at Lady Holland's. One day I may come back and hold you to your promise."

"I shall count on it. For now, I expect we had best hurry to Grosvenor Square. The caterers are generally reliable, but even a small wedding breakfast requires supervision."

In St. George's Street, passersby had stopped to cheer the nuptials. A pack of ragged children, always

203

alert to a Quality wedding, scrambled for the coins Jerry and Lord Heston were tossing out for good luck.

Clayburn was nowhere in sight.

Francesca told herself she was glad of it. Even the brief glimpse of him in the church had turned her bones to jelly. If compelled to exchange pleasantries with him, she would surely dissolve altogether.

She couldn't help but scan the pavement in both directions, though. Three carriages had already pulled up, ready to convey the wedding party to Grosvenor Square, and she longed to slip around them to see if he might be standing across the street.

Perhaps he would appear at the breakfast. But in the deepest part of her heart, she knew he would not.

Suddenly, she could not bear the shrieks of the children and Livvy's shrill laughter. Surrounded by other people's joy, she felt a crushing blow of self-pity. This will never be mine, she thought. And when Papa is gone, I shall be truly and forever alone.

While Maria's attention was diverted, she slipped back inside the church to regain her composure.

Sunlight streamed through the stained-glass windows over the altar, casting patterns of color on the wide flagstone aisle. An elderly verger snuffed the last candle and tottered into the sacristy, closing the door behind him.

In the empty silence, she knelt on the icy floor and summoned a prayer for Papa's health. But it was a false, mechanical prayer, because her thoughts immediately flew to Clayburn again.

Had she been wrong to send him away? What was the use of pride, when choosing it above all other things left her so miserable?

Weak, silly, *stupid* woman!

And yet the pain she felt now, she would have felt eventually. Suppose you had married him? she asked herself. How soon before he would have left to resume his former life—months? Weeks? It's better this way, and you'll accept that, when it doesn't hurt quite so much. He never loved you, after all. You are losing nothing that you might have had.

And then she saw him.

Trailing one hand along the carved wooden rail, he appeared from the shadows under the overhanging gallery and moved to stand before the enormous painting of Christ's Last Supper suspended over the altar.

Stunned, she could only gaze openmouthed at his back. His arms hung at his sides, and in one hand she saw something white, like a sheet of paper. He might have been a groom, except that he did not turn to watch his bride walk down the aisle.

To her horror, she realized that she was on her feet and those same feet were moving toward the aisle. Haltingly, to be sure, but they would not be stopped. She drew closer to the tall, silent figure, scarcely daring to breathe.

His head lifted, and she stopped immediately, but he only made a low sound in his throat. It echoed in the quiet church. Then his hand, the one holding the paper, swung in front of him and his head bent. After a few moments, she heard the slight hiss of paper being torn apart.

When his hand dropped again, a few small scraps were clutched between his fingers.

Like a tiny book, she thought, the memory striking her a second later. She had never thanked him for the book! It gave her a perfectly reasonable excuse to speak to him one last time. Her feet must have agreed, because they were moving again.

He heard her, she realized when he glanced over his shoulder. And then only his eyes moved, every color in the rainbow reflected from the startled, silver-mirror gaze. She gazed back, vaguely aware that she had stopped once more, close enough to touch him had they both reached out their hands.

Vibrant light poured over him from every direction, through the faces of saints and prophets, through the wings of archangels and the smiles of cherubs etched in the stained-glass windows. It glistened off his thick dark hair and turned his white collar and neckcloth to red and blue and green.

He seemed poised before her at the instant just before being thrust into hell, she thought, a bright angel who had cast his lot with Lucifer. Until this moment, she had not truly understood what he might once have been or could have become.

Such a horrific waste. But perhaps one day he would find a Mrs. Vertue, as Bromley had done. He might then be desperate enough to grasp a lifeline, however tenuous, and cling to it.

If only she could be the one to pull him to shore.

He had turned and was bowing. "Miss Childe. I thought you long since on your way with the others."

Panic slammed her then, transforming her curtsy into a rubbery bounce. She had to speak to him as if they were the merest of acquaintances. *Book,* she thought, grasping at her own lifeline. Thank him. Simple words. Few syllables.

"The book," she ventured cautiously. "I found it. That is, I assumed you meant to leave it. Should I have returned it to you?"

"I've no use for poetry," he replied, his expression hardening. "Of course you must keep it."

"Well, 'tis my father who wanted it, of course. I mean to give it to him, if you have no objection."

"Why should I? The book is yours. Feed it to the fire if you wish."

Like a hard slap across the face, his words jolted her from panic to temper. But she pressed the anger into the hard ball of other emotions knotted up inside her. This was the last time they would meet. She absolutely must not give in to hysterics. "Even John Hatchard could not discover its whereabouts," she said, keeping her voice even. "However did you find it?"

"In my usual fashion," he replied with a touch of sarcasm. "Drinking and gaming with the other scoundrels at Wolvercote. You recall that I returned there after delivering Livvy to the inn. Fallon lost a sum of money to me and was delighted to settle his debt with books in lieu of cash." He shrugged. "Naturally, I could not be sure I'd discovered the one you were seeking."

"You've had it in your possession all these weeks?"

"I was waiting for the perfect moment to present it to you, with accompanying flourishes." With a faint smile, he gazed at a spot over her shoulder. "Now, of course, I realize that such a moment was never to be."

She ran her tongue over dry lips. "The Petrarch is quite valuable, Lord Clayburn. I have no idea what Fallon owed to you when you accepted the book in exchange, but I shall gladly pay that amount or the book's market price, whichever sum is greater."

"God. It needed only this!"

For a long moment, the air fairly crackled around him. He stared at her with acute loathing. But when he spoke again, his voice had no expression at all. "I am aware you hold me in contempt, Miss Childe. With some reason, for in all my life I have done little of value and a great many things I regret. But I have never been my father's lackey. I do not covet your land or your fortune. And though I sought to win your affections by being of service to you, how is that a crime? I am a stranger to love. I could think of no other way to prove my sincerity. Dammit, what did you expect from a besotted fool? Love poems?"

With that, he strode swiftly past her.

Paralyzed, she heard the hollow beat of his shoes against the floor, growing fainter until the sound disappeared. Still she could not move. After a long while, she remembered to start breathing again.

Her mind was as incapable of thought as her body was of motion. She felt only a deep, burning emptiness where her heart had been and an aching sense of loss.

"Francesca?"

Dimly she recognized Maria's voice calling from the vestibule. Life must go on, she supposed. The wedding feast awaited.

Legs rigid, she turned and made her way slowly down the aisle, gaze focused on the worn stone paving where countless brides had joyously walked. Where minutes ago Clayburn had walked out of her life.

A scrap of paper, torn at the edges, lay starkly white against the gray stones just in front of her. Without thought she bent to pick it up, meaning to discard it later in a trash basket, and continued to where Maria waited with a concerned look on her face.

"Is everything all right, my dear? Clayburn stormed by a few moments ago, failing to acknowledge me when I called to him. Did something happen between the two of you?"

"Nothing of consequence," she replied, glancing at the bit of paper in her hand to avoid meeting her friend's eyes. There was writing on one side, the side that had been turned down so that she failed to notice it. Now, one word practically jumped from the page. *Francesca.*

Clayburn must have dropped this. She remembered the sound of paper tearing and the remnants clutched in his hand as they spoke. A letter, perhaps? One he had decided not to send?

Heart pounding, she suggested that Maria proceed to the carriage. "I'll f-follow shortly," she promised.

Obviously worried, Maria nodded and left Francesca alone in the shadowy vestibule.

With trembling hands she lifted the fragment of paper to the light from the open door and read the few, broken lines.

Precious God. He had written her a poem!

She recognized the faltering rhymes, the commonplace images, the earnest struggle to wrench feelings into words. Papa had written poetry like this to Renalda, deplorable as literature but incandescent with love.

To think Clayburn had done the same. For *her*! In her wildest, most fantastical dreams, she could never have imagined that rakehell huddled over paper and an inkpot, composing verses to "beloved Francesca, goddess mine . . ."

Wings attached themselves to her feet. She all but flew outside, unsurprised to catch no sight of him. Only one carriage remained on the street, Maria standing beside the open door.

"Which way did he go?" she demanded.

Without hesitation, Maria pointed south.

Lifting her skirts, Francesca set off at a run, dodging pedestrians and veering into the gutter when necessary. For once glad of her height, she searched for a glimpse of his broad shoulders and dark hair over the stream of men and women about their Saturday morning errands. No sign of him.

She turned right at Conduit Street and shortly after dashed in front of a hackney to go left on Bond Street. Instinct drove her on. She had no rational idea where he was headed, but never doubted she would find him.

209

And sure enough, across the next street and midway down the block after that, she saw a tall man poised on the curbside, arm lifted to hail a hack. His hair shone in the sunlight as if on fire.

Summoning a new burst of speed, she darted across the intersection in defiance of the oncoming traffic, fractionally aware of a rider screaming oaths at her as his horse reared up. A brewer's dray careened into a streetlamp.

Ignoring the chaos in her wake, she ran even faster when a hackney pulled up in front of him. His hand went to the door latch.

Still a block to go! She could not reach him in time. "Clayburn! Wait!"

He must not have heard her. He already had one foot on the floorboard when she shoved herself between a large woman and her equally pudgy companion, all but knocking them to the ground.

"Clayburn!" she shrieked.

He turned, poised halfway between pavement and coach, an astonished look on his face.

She pelted the last few yards and hurled herself at his chest.

Just in time, he opened his arms to catch her. Only his strength held her upright. Her legs had cramped up, dangling uselessly from her body as she sucked huge mouthfuls of air into her burning lungs.

"I . . . found . . ." She panted. "Don't . . . go . . . please."

"I'm here," he said. "Breathe slowly, Francesca. That's good." His fingers massaged her back. "Relax. We have all the time in the world."

"No. Don't have . . . time. N-now! Here!"

"Whatever you say, my—"

"That's right, guv'nor," a voice shouted.

"Go on, dearie," said a woman from directly behind her. "You tell 'im. We won't let the bloke get away."

As the world stopped spinning in dizzy circles around her, she became aware of the fascinated crowd gathering to enjoy what promised to be an interesting spectacle.

She didn't care if everyone in England listened in, so long as Clay was among them. Nor could she stop the flood of tears pouring down her cheeks.

"I'm s-so s-sorry," she sobbed into his neckcloth. "I did everything all wr-wrong. You were so good. So very good to me. But I wouldn't *see*! I just c-couldn't believe, even though I wanted to. *Because* I wanted to."

"See what?" he asked softly. "Believe what?"

"That you might really l-love me."

A few onlookers hissed at Clayburn. "You blind?" one of them called. "She's a beauty!"

"I'll take 'er, iffen you don't want 'er," a male voice offered. There was a scuffle as someone objected to the man's impertinence, likely with a fist, from the thud and cry of pain that followed.

Francesca lifted her face, scarcely daring to look into Clayburn's eyes. He had indulged her fits of temper and emotional displays so many times. She feared he was doing the same now, no more than that, only until she was calm enough to be dismissed in a civilized manner.

But he gazed back at her with gentle curiosity. "Whyever did you think I could not love you?" he asked. "Is it because I lived a stupid life before we met? To be sure, falling in love with you is the only intelligent thing I've ever done. No wonder you are surprised."

"N-not your life before. That was the excuse. Your father was another excuse. I had thousands of excuses to hold you away, and fought you because it was easier than fighting myself. But all the time, it's been *me*!" She clutched at his coat with both hands. "I'm too tall, and I don't know how to go on in London Society, and I'm a m-mongrel by birth. And worst of all, I'm *o-ol-older* than you!"

Mortified, she buried her face against his lapels and heard a low rumble from his chest. Good God. He was laughing!

"You omitted your hair-trigger temper," he reminded her fiendishly. "And your resolution to manage everyone who crosses your path, and your remarkable ability to flay a man with your tongue from thirty paces. But *older* than I? Perhaps when we began, before I became entangled with you and Bromley and Arthur and the fearsome Livvy. But I swear I've aged a decade in the last few weeks."

"Wretch," she scolded into his neckcloth. "Years of dissipation brought you down. We Childes only speeded the process."

"I say you marry her!" a woman exclaimed.

The crowd took up the chant. *"Marry her! Marry her!"*

"It seems we must humor the masses," he said, prying her gently from his chest and standing her back a few inches so that he could look into her eyes. His lips curved in a beautiful smile. "For no other reason than because we both want it, Francesca, will you be my wife?"

A hush fell over the street. Everyone leaned forward to hear her answer.

"Oh, yes," she whispered.

To loud cheers, he pulled her firmly into his arms and gave her a lingering kiss.

Then, breathless, she felt him lift her into the coach. A flower peddler stepped forward and pressed a bouquet of March daffodils into his hands.

"For the bride," she said with a toothless smile.

Clayburn spoke to the jarvey, jumped inside, and waved out the window as the carriage pulled away. Then he tossed the flowers onto the squabs, seized Francesca by the waist, and pulled her onto his lap. "We shall be the talk of the neighborhood over supper tonight."

"Where are we going now?" she asked, toying with a vagrant swatch of dark hair over his ear.

"Why, to Grosvenor Square, of course. Are you not the hostess for a wedding breakfast? Not ours, alas. But everyone will be concerned if you fail to appear."

"The devil with them all!" she declared, surprising another laugh from him. "But I suppose we must."

"Not to quibble with my great good fortune, love, but what exactly sent you chasing after me of a sudden? Certainly nothing I said to you in that church."

"You were beastly," she agreed, "which I roundly deserved. But it's what you wrote that opened my eyes at last. And my heart." She held out her right hand and realized it was empty. "Oh God. I've lost it! I must have dropped it in the street. We must go back and find it."

"We'll do nothing of the sort," he said tranquilly. "Whatever it was, I shall replace it. What precisely did you lose?"

"The poem! The one you wrote for me. The one you tore up by the altar. On your way out, one piece fell from your hand. I found it, and saw my name and read the words."

"A wonder you did not run in the other direction, then. I am no poet. Obviously."

"I don't care! I mean, I could hardly tell from the little that I found, but you must show me all of it."

"One day," he agreed, color washing over his cheeks.

"Not soon. As of now, I am three lines short of a sonnet and fourteen lines short of a decent one. But in a few years' time, when I've polished it up, perhaps I'll read it to you." He grinned. "You might have had the decency to be christened with a name I could rhyme."

"Lots of words rhyme with Francesca," she retorted. "But you'll need to learn Italian."

"Gladly. You can teach me." He untied the ribbons of her bonnet and sent it to join the daffodils. "Meantime, I'll not allow you the slightest opportunity to change your mind again. We are solemnly and very publicly betrothed to each other."

"I won't change my mind," she vowed. "I have only just found it, you know."

He gave her an uncertain smile. "Does your mind perchance tell you that you are in love with me?"

"Oh yes. My heart, too. And the rest of my body is shouting Amen."

She'd meant to make him laugh, but he only applied himself intently to the buttons of her pelisse, his expression unreadable. If she didn't know better, she would have thought her consummately sophisticated rake was having an attack of shyness. After a moment, she took his hands away and began to peel off his gloves. "You are supposed to be happy that I love you, Lord Clayburn."

His gaze met hers and held. "Never doubt it, Francesca. I'm a bit dazed is all. It suddenly hit me like a shot from a crossbow, you here with me, meaning to stay with me, *wanting* to. As many times as I dreamed this and told myself it would come to pass, I must not have believed it."

"Cupid has taken to firing a *crossbow*?"

That did make him smile. With gloves off, he made swift work of unbuttoning her pelisse and removing it. "I believe you should tell me a dozen times each day that you love me, if it's not too much trouble. And my first name is Galen, although only my mother has ever used it. I hope you will not."

"Do you prefer Clay? Unless I'm in a temper, of course, in which case there is no telling what I'll call you." She gave him an assessing look. "Are you altogether certain you wish to spend the rest of your life with a tinderbox?"

"Goddess of fire," he corrected softly. "And yes, I have been certain for a very long time. The question has always been, would you take a scoundrel to your heart?"

"Oh, you scoundrels have a way of pushing your way in, and a good thing, too." She brushed away another tear before it could fall. "Thank you, Clay, for not giving up on me."

He drew her into his arms and held her in a strong, silent embrace that told her more than words could explain. She felt him sealing her to himself with fierce possession and respect. And love. In those minutes, she thought as he gently set her back again, they had pledged themselves to each other. She looked into his eyes and knew he was thinking the same thing.

"It's done, then," she said.

"Yes." He smiled. "Long past time, if you ask me. There are the formalities to be got through, of course, and a few details to be settled. Most can wait, but is there anything you wish to discuss now, while we are alone?"

He knew her so well. "My father," she murmured, fumbling with the lapels of his greatcoat. "His letters say that his health is much improved, and he even enclosed a note from his physician to back him up, but I cannot leave him alone any longer. I'm all he has, you see."

"On the contrary, my love. He's about to be saddled

with a son-in-law. Perhaps a grandchild within the year. I certainly mean to do *my* part. You wish to live with him, yes?"

"Will you mind? We are talking about Rutland-shire, Clay. The back of beyond. It will be you and me and Papa and the sheep."

"Far better company than I've kept the last many years," he said with a laugh. "But there is one thing more, if you will. I should like to bring my mother into our home. She has lost all sense of herself under Montford's rule, and—"

"Most certainly she is welcome! As for your father, we'll not give up hope of him altogether. Maria Beaton advised me to burn no bridges, so let us leave one open for him to cross. Happiness has a way of disappearing if it is not shared."

"Well, then. So far as I am concerned, the whole world is invited to share with us. Meantime, I under-stand you have planned to leave for home tomorrow morning. We'll travel together, me riding outside the coach for propriety's sake. Separate rooms at the inn, for the same reason. I'd prefer to overnight at the Rose and Thistle where we first met, if you have no objection."

"N-none." She couldn't for the life of her put two coherent words together as he began to remove the pins from her hair.

"When we arrive at Sotherton Manor," he con-tinued, "I shall quite properly ask the duke's per-mission to approach his daughter with an offer of marriage. I rely on you to convince him this is a good idea. Then I mean to go before you on bended knee with a well-rehearsed proposal, which I expect you to accept. After that, you may decide where, when, and with what ceremony we are to be legally wed. I vote for immediately."

His fingers combed through her hair. "God, how I've longed to do this." He lifted his hand. "Look, you. I am shaking like a rattle."

"No more than I," she said, seizing his hand and bringing it to her lips. "But how can you speak of propriety when I am sitting on your lap with my hair down and—" She squealed as his other hand began to roam up her leg, lifting her skirt as it went.

He took a moment to examine what his hand had uncovered. "Long, sleek, and bewitching. Exactly as I imagined."

"I th-thought we were going to the wedding breakfast, Clay."

"Why, so we are. And when we arrive, I mean to transform myself into a model gentleman. But I instructed the jarvey to take us the long way around. A *very* long way around."

"Oh my," she protested halfheartedly as he toyed with her garter. "But you can't mean to . . . here . . . in a *hackney*!"

"Well, perhaps not quite. We'll save the best for our wedding night." He brushed a kiss on her cheek, and another, moving closer and closer to her lips. "But for one brief hour more, beloved, I want to be a scoundrel and do wicked things with you."

"Yes, please," she murmured as his hand moved past her garter, heading north. "But why an hour? You may go on being wicked forever, Lord Rakehell, so long as it's only with me."

About the Author

Lynn Kerstan is the winner of the 1996 RITA Award for Best Regency Romance for *Gwen's Christmas Ghost*, which she coauthored with Alicia Rasley. The RITA is awarded annually by the Romance Writers of America.

Lynn Kerstan loves to hear from readers. You may write to her at P.O. Box 182301, Coronado, CA 92178-2301 or send e-mail to lynnkerstan@poboxes.com.